Rebury - Text copyright © Emmy Ellis 2024
Cover Art by Emmy Ellis @ studioenp.com © 2024

All Rights Reserved

Rebury is a work of fiction. All characters, places, and events are from the author's imagination. Any resemblance to persons, living or dead, events or places is purely coincidental.

The author respectfully recognises the use of any and all trademarks.

With the exception of quotes used in reviews, this book may not be reproduced or used in whole or in part by any means existing without written permission from the author.

Warning: The unauthorised reproduction or distribution of this copyrighted work is illegal. No part of this book may be scanned, uploaded, or distributed via the Internet or any other means, electronic or print, without the author's written permission.

REBURY

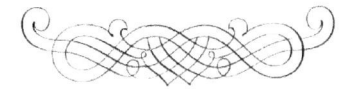

Emmy Ellis

Chapter One

Father Michael Donovan looked after Our Lady of St Patrick's, and he'd agreed to do so now under The Brothers' protection when they'd approached him a month ago—although he didn't have to pay them any money, they paid him. They'd also offered the same deal to St Thomas', the church where bodies had been discovered a while back. He made the sign of the cross (it had been such a shocking time) and hoped no such thing happened in *his* sanctuary.

He ought to be horrified as to what the twins got up to, but as he'd discovered during a chat with them, underneath it all they were kind men with big hearts. He most definitely didn't agree with some of their rumoured methods but would turn a blind eye. The loose roof tiles were being repaired today. Tomorrow, a Christmas fayre, completely funded by George and Greg, which would bring in much-needed funds. Michael was turning a blind eye to *that*, too.

George especially was sick of not knowing what certain people were up to behind their backs (Michael hadn't asked what that had meant and he never would), so the fayre was a way for them to chat with their residents and let them know that grassing to them wasn't exactly grassing, it was more keeping the community safe. Michael knew exactly what they were really doing, but if he didn't voice it out loud he could claim innocence. For so long his church had been a quarter full, people's faith dwindling, and he'd love it to be bursting to the rafters every Sunday again, which it could be with the twins' help.

They'd promised to fund free tea, coffee, soft drinks, sandwiches, and cakes after every service. Those who were down on their uppers would come for the food and perhaps take on board the sermons, which in turn would mean they'd live better lives.

That was Michael's wish anyway.

"Yes, they're decent men," he reminded himself—or was that God he tried to convince?—tidying his desk in the vestry.

He was good at convincing himself of things for the better of his flock. So long as George and Greg didn't tell him of murders or illegal goings-on, God would forgive him for being in cahoots with them.

The little bell above the main door tinkled, so he left the vestry and went to see who'd come in. A woman ventured up the aisle, and going by her jerky movements, she was unsure whether she should be there. She seemed worn down but not down on her luck—she appeared to have money, she could afford to eat, so something else must be troubling her.

"Can I help you?" he asked on his approach.

"I…" She stopped walking and bit her lip, placing one hand on the back of a pew. She glanced around, her gaze stopping on the exit as though she contemplated going back outside, never to return.

"Would you like a minute?" He'd said it gently to coax her to stay.

She turned to look at him and sank onto the pew, her eyes welling with tears that fell over her cheeks. "I'm at my wit's end. I don't know what to do."

"Would you like confession or just a chat?" Michael was mindful that she may have information the twins would need to know. Yes, he'd also agreed to be their ears and had no guilt about that whatsoever. If they could help, then he'd tell them what he thought they needed to know.

"A chat would be lovely," she said.

"If you're okay with me locking the door so we're not disturbed, we can talk in the vestry. I have a kettle there and can make you some tea."

She nodded, not a flicker of fear at the idea of being alone with him. Not for the first time, Michael noted how people automatically trusted a man or woman of God, when sadly, in this devious day and age, they maybe shouldn't.

"You're safe here." He took his bunch of keys from his pocket, securing the door and returning to her. "Come on then. One sugar or two?"

She smiled. "Sod it, I'll have two." Then she blushed. "Sorry. I swore."

He smiled back, thinking of how George had been effing and jeffing the last time they'd paid him a visit. "I'd rather you be yourself so you can relax. A bit of swearing didn't hurt anyone."

He led her to the vestry and gestured to one of his big comfortable armchairs, the one with the tartan cushions. He flicked the kettle on and washed two cups up in his little sink in the kitchenette corner. He kept his back to her to give her time to become comfortable here. "Start at the beginning or even the middle or end. Get it off your chest."

"It's my son," she said.

He imagined him dying or in trouble with the law and all manner of scenarios. He'd heard them all. "Go on then."

She told him a story about a good boy who'd turned bad, or not so much bad but he'd wandered down the wrong path. He took drugs and expected her to fund his habit, and he'd been stealing from her, items from the house that he must have sold on.

Michael passed her a cup of tea and took his to sit on the other armchair. He found putting himself behind the desk meant the wooden barrier between him and parishioners created an emotional divide—he wanted them to think of him as a friend, not an authoritative figure.

"You said you've tried to get him to go for help and that you'd pay for it. Why do you think he doesn't want to do that?"

"Because the drugs have got hold of him too hard. All he can think about is his next hit." She took a tissue out of her pocket and wiped her runny nose. "I'm here because I hate the way I feel."

"What do you mean?"

"I'm his mother and should want to help him right until the end, but I'm so tired and want to give up and let him get on with it by himself. I shouldn't want to do that."

"Is he an adult?"

"Yes. He's been fucking me about since he was sixteen."

"That's quite a burden to carry. You can't help your feelings. It sounds as if he has no regard for them, he's intent on getting what he needs. You have to ask yourself about *your* needs. There's an element of being cruel to be kind. The problem is, because he's no longer a child, it would be difficult for you to insist a doctor helps him. That's not me saying you should have gone for help before now, I understand that every situation is different and events dictate what you do and don't do. We have to look at this problem where it sits now. Are you prepared to still have him living with you?"

"That's not an issue. He left ages ago."

"Where did he go?"

"He moved in with some friends from college, the ones who got him into this mess in the first place. It doesn't look like he's eating much. He's lost a lot of weight. He comes to my work at about five in the morning and asks for money. My old boss would have been angry if he'd seen him there. But he died, and now I have two new bosses who might be violent towards him if they catch him loitering around."

Michael's stomach rolled over. Was it possible, because she'd said *two* new bosses, that she referred to the twins? "Who are your bosses?"

She sipped her tea as if in contemplation, a 'should I answer or not?' situation. She moved forward to place her cup on a coaster on the desk, leaning back to close her eyes for a moment. Her burden weighed heavy, that much was obvious. "The Brothers."

Oh dear. I'll have to be careful what I say here. "Let's look at this rationally. Why do you think they'd hurt your son because he's outside your work? Other than that, he takes drugs, you haven't said he harms you, he's driven you to your limit, so why would that need violence? Would they not see it as an opportunity to help him get off the drugs? They have fearsome reputations, and the rumours about them are awful, but I can read people, and they're decent underneath. Would you like me to talk to them on your behalf and explain? I wouldn't tell them who you are—how can I when you haven't even told me your name?"

"That's what I've been wondering. I know them well enough to approach them myself, but my problem is that they like me and might take offence that my son's treating me badly—and more to the point, that I came here for help first instead of going to them."

"Unless your lad has moved to another Estate, then he's their resident and they may want to help."

She twisted her fingers together. "I don't know. Maybe what I used to do for a living… Maybe this is all karma. Maybe I deserve to suffer."

She hadn't said it in a pity-me way, more stating how she felt. Michael considered her to be a strong woman who'd found herself floundering, the emotions attached to this situation what she struggled with the most. She'd perhaps asked herself how a mother could turn her back on her son at the point he needed her the most. But how could that mother continue on when that son didn't *want* her help? Catch twenty-two.

"We can fix this either way," Michael said. "Well, we might not be able to fix him, but we could fix *you* to some degree. He *does* need help, but we can't force a horse to drink the water."

"Are you saying he's a lost cause?"

"No, just that he's got to want to get himself off the drugs and at the moment he doesn't. There's no tougher subject than someone who refuses to see."

She sighed. Was she annoyed he didn't have the answer she'd come here for, the magic wand he'd wave to make it all better? He wished he could do that, but unfortunately, he'd learned it wasn't always possible to change certain situations.

"What did you mean about what you did for a living and karma?"

"I sold my body, and now I work somewhere overseeing other women who do the same thing. My son never made me feel guilty about what I did until he met those boys. Honestly, it's as if the Devil is inside him now."

Michael thought she'd said that because it was what many a priest would say, but he wasn't of the mind that the actual Devil got inside human beings. Teenage rebellion, wanting to be accepted and part of a crowd, hormones, and bad life choices were what had happened. He'd seen it many times over, and there was hope: lots of people hooked on drugs ended up living a clean life.

"What's he taking?" he asked.

"It started off with smoking weed, then heroin in with it, and now I think he's injecting."

"Such a sad state of affairs when one so promising and with a full future trips over, and that's all he's done. He's tripped over and can't get back up again on his own. It needs someone to be able to get through to him, to the old part of him that used to listen. I appreciate how difficult that is. You said yourself you've tried hundreds of times. What do you feel about helping him feed his addiction? What has playing your part in that done to you? I'm by no means blaming you because I fully understand why you did it — seeing a child in pain, even if it's from drug withdrawal, must be awful. You thought you were doing the right thing. But do you acknowledge that it wasn't?"

"God, yes. If I'd stayed strong in the beginning and hadn't given him money, I don't think it would have gone this far."

"But on the other hand, it might have. He turned to stealing, and he'd have done that sooner if you'd refused to give him cash. He's chosen to do what he's done. He's the one who must face up to the responsibility of that like you've faced up to your role in this. Let's put aside your guilt and focus on the outcome. If he comes to your work or your home and demands money again, and you refuse again, what do you think will happen?"

"He had a knife last time. I managed to persuade him not to use it on me. And he'll get drugs on tick, he's done it before. He'll steal from someone else."

"Then that's his decision, too. Tell him you'll be there to support him by *talking* if he decides to get off drugs, or even if he chooses to stay on them, but you'll no longer be the Bank of Mum." He held a hand up to stop her protest. "I know it sounds as if you're abandoning him, but you're not. You're there for emotional support. You haven't turned him away."

"But what if he steals from the wrong person? Or owes the wrong drug runner? Or takes too much and overdoses? I'll be left with the guilt."

"From someone else's actions as well as your own. I understand. Would he come here to talk to me?"

She laughed bitterly. "I didn't bring him up in the faith. I stopped going to church when I became pregnant. My father made me feel as though God would be angry that I was having a baby without being married, so I walked away to save being even more disappointed in myself than I already was. If I didn't visit God's house every week then I wouldn't feel *His* disappointment."

"So you were brought up a Catholic?"

"Yes."

"I suspect you've already gone back into the past and told yourself off. If I hadn't had a baby, then that baby wouldn't have grown up to take drugs."

She nodded. "I've beaten myself up every step of the way. I tried so hard to provide for him to prove to everybody I could do it. Until he was sixteen, I'd done a really good job."

"Until he made his own life choices. You shouldn't be held responsible for what he's opted to do."

"But I do."

"I know, and that's the cross you'll bear. While I feel for him, you're my main priority. You're the one who's reached out, the one I can actually help. We can talk as much and as often as you need to, until you've accepted that just as you walked on your own path, your son is doing the same."

"I can never turn my back on him like my dad did to me."

"You don't have to. Just be there to walk beside him on his journey, although I appreciate that will be painful for you. Always remind him that there *is* an alternative, that he can stop what he's doing with help and live that life he wanted before he met those people. All isn't lost. Are you on social media?"

She frowned. "What's that got to do with anything?"

"I was going to mention all of the memes that talk about the subject of starting again, and it's never too late. So many people follow their life's calling years down the line after making mistakes. He can do it, too, but he has to want to."

"It's so complicated. My old boss was a drug dealer. Honestly, I'm not a bad person, I didn't imagine I'd hang around with people like that, it's just the way it happened. When he died, someone else took over the drug-selling side of his business, and I have a feeling my son's working for him now. I can't be sure, it's just something he said. He mentioned the new dealer's name, which isn't a common one, so I might have put two and two together and made five."

"And is this conducted on Cardigan?"

"Yes."

"Perhaps the twins *should* be told."

"They know the dealer's working on their patch, so he isn't technically doing anything wrong. He has their permission. I'm worried that my old boss' right-hand man will get involved if my son does something wrong, like steal drugs he's supposed to be selling."

"What are their names?"

"If I tell you, you'll let the twins know, won't you."

"If that's what you want."

She sighed. "Cooper and Boycie. But please, explain to George and Greg that my lad has got a bit lost, he isn't a bad kid."

"Then I'll need his name, too."

She took a deep breath and picked up her tea. "Ezra Darlington. I'm Elizabeth—Betty—but they know me as Widow." She blinked, tears falling. "Oh God, what have I done?"

Chapter Two

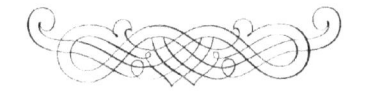

If she hadn't been kicked out of the family home by her dad for being pregnant, she'd never be standing in this old-fashioned house in an old-fashioned dress. Every sex worker was required to act as though they were from another time, depending on which outfit they chose. Elizabeth Darlington was Betty to her friends but Widow to the punters—she'd chosen the

role of a woman in mourning who shockingly didn't observe the rules of grief in the Victorian times; she didn't wear black and had sex with anyone she wanted. Every night at work was a performance, the same one acted out over and over again but with different men.

The big manor house had once been abandoned and left to rot until a rich American woman, Indiana, had bought it. She'd given it a facelift, and each room resembled an era from the past. Betty's favourite was the one with the red brocade wallpaper, a real boudoir with the black curtains and matching bedspread.

She sat in the large kitchen where everyone gathered at shift change. The daytime girls passed on any concerns so the night-time ladies were aware. They all drank tea and had a laugh, and some who'd become good friends traded stories and secrets. Betty's best friend and next-door neighbour, Lainey, sat across the other side of the room, so Betty joined in a chat with some of the others.

"How's your son doing at college?" Lioness asked.

Betty didn't particularly want to talk about Ezra. He'd started smoking weed, maybe even doing much worse, getting in with the wrong crowd. He'd called her a slag the other day—she'd always been open with what she did for a living, obviously not getting graphic about it, but he knew she worked in the big house called the Bordello. As he'd grown older, he'd possibly heard rumours about what went on there, and at sixteen he'd turned into quite the little twat. Gone was the nice boy, and someone else had taken his place, striding so easily into his life and taking it over. Nothing she said was right at the moment. He bit her head off more often than not.

"Oh, he's fine," Betty said. "You know boys, they become secretive as they get older, don't want anything to do with their mothers." Except when it came to asking her for money.

"Typical kids. They hang around your arse for years and then all of a sudden can't stand the sight of you." Lioness sighed. "My daughter's the same. Seventeen and thinks she knows it all, but then so did I at that age."

Betty thought back to when she was seventeen, pregnant with Ezra and worried about her future when Dad had kicked her out. She'd gone into sex work not long after her son had been born, a friend of hers telling her about it. Luckily, Betty hadn't started on the streets but had gone straight into a brothel in a four-bed house, taught how to work and how to handle the customers, her environment safe, and the only time she'd felt fear at work was when that weirdo had been going round strangling women like her, almost to the point they died, then he'd claimed it was a kink game.

No one in her street knew how she earned a living except Lainey. She'd told the babysitter, when she'd had one, she worked in a factory, doing nights because of the double pay. The sitter was a couple of years younger than Betty, a sister to four younger brothers, so she knew what she was doing. She'd studied while Ezra slept, and the arrangement had worked for everyone for years.

Until Ezra had turned thirteen and didn't want a babysitter anymore. He'd said he could look after himself, didn't need Sarah 'hanging around', as he'd put it. Sarah hadn't had kids at that point, she'd lived to work and study, and although it meant she'd lost the weekly wage Betty had paid her, she'd said it would be nice to have her evenings at home instead.

It brought a whole new set of worries to Betty's doorstep three years later. Neighbours phoned her mobile to say parties were going on in her house every Friday night or Ezra was hanging around in the street being uncharacteristically loud and obnoxious with his friends. College had certainly changed him, she didn't recognise him anymore, and it saddened her that she'd done so well, what with being a teenage mother when she'd had him, and now it was going to look as if people's predictions had come true. He'd turned into a no-good little fucker, and she was going to get the blame. With no boyfriend there to provide extra parental support, she faced Ezra alone.

She was getting pretty tired of it, and something needed to give.

Lioness had drifted away, likely gathering that Betty had gone off in her head again. The daytime shift were on their way out of the kitchen, the night-time workers standing to put their cups in the dishwasher. Indiana declared everyone should have a good night and disappeared into her office. Widow wanted a job like hers one day, to be the person who ran things and didn't have to open her legs. Not that that kind of job would make Ezra happier because she'd still be around other 'sluts'. She'd have to retrain as a secretary or something to stop him from looking down his nose at her.

She sighed and placed her cup on the rack, and as she was the last one, she put the dishwasher on a quick cycle. She popped the lids on the biscuit tins dotted on the table, then stacked them on the worktop. She loved this place and everyone who worked here. They'd become her family, this house as familiar as her own. At least people here were more welcoming. Whenever she arrived home at half two every morning, if Ezra was still awake, she sensed the scorn coming off him. The thing was, he might hate her job and think she was a slag, but he never had a problem asking for the money being a slag provided.

Funny that.

Music filtered through, so she quickly went to the ballroom. Several other women chatted to punters who they'd soon take upstairs. The Bordello gave the illusion a party was held here every night, and everyone pretended they'd only just met their customer, chatting away and having a glass of bubbly. Some had a dance before going upstairs, but there was a fifteen-minute rule of acting like they were getting to know each other, then the deed had to be done.

Betty approached her six-fifteen customer, recognising him because of his Phantom of the Opera mask. He usually fucked her from behind. A few punters did that, probably because of the guilt. If they didn't see a face while they had sex, they could convince themselves they weren't cheating.

"Evening," he said as she approached him.

She'd always had the idea his visits here were meant to be a secret. Maybe him wearing the mask gave him the sense he wasn't really doing this, but whatever, she was curious about him. There was some underlying *'thing' she couldn't quite grasp with him. Menace? Was he prone to violence?*

"Good evening." She smiled, then following the house rules, said, "Do you come here often?"

"I do. I wanted to ask you something but wasn't sure what your answer would be."

"Why don't you ask it anyway? You might be surprised by my response."

"We should move into the corner."

She followed him there, intrigued as to whether he was playing the game or if this was a serious question. "Go on then, I'm listening."

"If what I'm about to say isn't up your alley, walk away and we won't discuss it again." There was that hint of menace. "But if it is, then that will be the pair of us pleased."

She frowned. "It's all very cryptic…"

He leaned close so she was pressed into the corner, his mouth to her ear. "I've got this house called the Orange Lantern. I want it done up similar to this place, right down to the wallpaper and curtains. And I want you to become my Indiana, running it for me. It hasn't done too well so far; it needs a proper manager, even though my mate thinks she can be one. We'll discuss the ins and outs if you're interested."

She had to make sure the career move was affordable. Plus, she didn't even know this man except for the fact he'd used her for sex. And what if this was a trick? Indiana might be testing her employees for trustworthiness and loyalty.

"How much are we talking?" she asked. "Per week."

He whispered an amount that had her eyes widening. "So what do you think?"

"I think, despite that wage, I'd be a fool to say yes until I'd seen the place and we'd discussed how it was going to work. Plus, I'd need to speak to Indiana because your house might be in direct competition with hers, and I wouldn't want to be involved in fucking her over."

He laughed. "Where do you think I got the idea from? She's given me tips and told me you were the ideal boss to run it. Go and ask her. I'll wait."

She strutted away and walked towards Indiana's office, working out how she was going to put this. Hi, I'm letting you know that I'm thinking about fucking off and leaving you, but can you give me confirmation this bloke is legit before I kick you in the teeth? *It didn't exactly sound nice when she put it like that, but that was basically what she was doing, wasn't it?*

She tapped on the door, her stomach rolling.

"Come in," Indiana called.

Betty went inside and blurted, "Some bloke's said you think I'd be a good fit to run his brothel. Is that right? Have I done something wrong so you want to get rid of me?"

Indiana smiled and pushed her chair back a little so she could rest her bare heels on the desk. The woman rarely put shoes on. "More like I want you to further your career. This is a great opportunity for you. Think about it, no sex, yet you'll be earning more. His business model is sound, I've talked it through with him."

Betty closed the door and moved forward to sit on the other side of the desk. "But isn't it going to affect the Bordello?"

"I doubt it very much. People who come here choose this place because it's so specific in what goes on. He may be stealing the wallpaper idea, but that's about it. It'll be a different type of customer. Why don't you go to the house and have a look tonight?"

"I can't afford to lose any pay." My son's nabbing money off me like it's going out of fashion.

"Which is why I've told him he'll have to give you cash before you step foot outside this building." Indiana folded her arms over her belly. "I was like you

once. Before I moved here from America, I was stuck in a rut, couldn't see any way out. Then when a client left me all of his money, I found this house and started the business. I could have lived off the inheritance, I could have given up work, but having been one of those women, desperate to make a wage every day, I wanted to help others do the same. Pay it forward. Now it's your turn."

"I'm a bit uneasy going off with someone I barely know."

"Then I'll come with you." Indiana took her feet off the desk and slipped them into soft-soled shoes. She walked out of the office, holding the door open for Betty to exit, then she locked it.

Betty followed her to the lady who manned the cloakroom and acted as a receptionist.

"We're popping out for an hour or two," Indiana said. "Any problems, give me a ring." She turned to Betty. "Go and let him know what's going on."

Betty found him in the corner of the ballroom. "Indiana said she'll come with us now to see the house and talk business, but I want paying first. I'll be losing cash tonight by going with you, and so will she. I'll need to pay her cut."

"Why do we have to go tonight? Tomorrow in the daytime means it wouldn't cost me anything because you wouldn't be at work."

"It's tonight or not at all."

"Fuck's sake, fair enough." He took his wallet out, counted a wedge, and passed it to her.

She stuck it inside her bra and led the way. In Indiana's car, they tailed him to the other side of the Cardigan Estate to a secluded street. The house wasn't as big as the Bordello, it had maybe ten bedrooms, but she could understand why he'd called it what he had. An orange lightbulb inside a lantern by the front door glowed brightly.

They all met on the garden path, and she found it a bit odd that he still had the Phantom mask on.

"Aren't you going to take that off?" she asked him as he slid the key in the lock.

"No, and I'll always have a mouth mask and sunglasses on in the future."

"What for?"

"No one I work with knows what I look like—apart from two people."

"And what do I call you? Boss?"

"No, Roach."

Her stomach dipped, and she thought she might be sick.

He sniffed. "I gather you've already heard of me."
She nodded.
He stared at her. "Is that going to be a problem?"

For you, when I find the courage to slice your fucking throat for supplying weed and fuck knows what else to my son.

She smiled nicely. "No, no problem at all."

Chapter Three

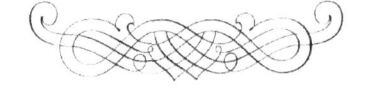

Betty left the church much lighter on one hand but even more burdened on the other. Father Donovan had made a lot of sense; he hadn't told her anything she hadn't already contemplated. Yes, she understood Ezra had made his own choices, but as his mother, she felt responsible for not only him but her part in this mess. If only his name-calling with regard to her profession didn't upset her so much, then she wouldn't try to make it all better by handing over wads of cash. To what, make him like her again? She was guilty of needing his approval, and if that meant giving him what he wanted, then she'd stupidly done it.

It was only now that things had got so much worse she realised her mistake. She'd made a rod for her own back and should have been stronger, but not wanting to turn out like her father had governed her actions. She wasn't a good parent—no matter that she'd brought Ezra up impeccably until he was sixteen, she'd failed after that.

I enabled him. And that was the crushing truth of the matter.

What she hadn't told Father Donovan was that she knew damn well Ezra worked for Cooper, it wasn't a suspicion at all. She'd followed him one evening, had seen him passing wraps to kids in that stupid secret handshake that wasn't fucking secret—everyone knew what it meant, what was going on, so these runners, if they thought they were being clever, weren't. She hadn't been able to confess fully—who'd want a priest frowning down on them? Although that wasn't fair. Father Donovan hadn't been reproachful at all, he'd seemed to understand her part in this and why she'd done it.

What people didn't tell you when you became a parent was that you didn't miraculously know it all, you were still learning yourself, winging it as you went along. Maybe she shouldn't beat herself up for making wrong decisions when there was no rule book to follow. What she'd actually followed was her heart and emotions, even though she'd known, deep down, giving him money was the wrong thing to do. She *had* tried to get him to go to a rehab centre, but he didn't want to know. It was a case of closing the stable door after the horse had bolted right into the sodding horizon. She should have locked her colt up as soon as he'd got into drugs and not let him out until the craving left him. But wouldn't that have been illegal? Wicked?

"Fucking hell," she muttered, getting into her car then sitting there staring at the open greenery of the park ahead.

Despite it being winter, people milled around the fountain and some fed the ducks. Others walked at a brisk pace. They all must have worries of their own, but at this moment hers seemed bigger than any they could be suffering.

She was drowning in remorse and wished she'd been so much stronger.

She sighed and got back out of the car. A walk might do her some good, so she joined the others in the park, starting with a lap around the small lake. She tucked her hands in her coat pockets and waited for her phone to ring, the twins on the other end of the line. Like she'd thought earlier, George would be upset she hadn't gone directly to him. She was brought out of her self-recrimination at the sight of one of her ex-customers from the Bordello. Shit.

"How are you, Widow?" he asked, getting control of his overexuberant spaniel. "I've missed you."

No, you've missed my hole. That was uncharitable but true all the same. "How are you?" She actually didn't want to know, but in this kind of situation she was trapped into making conversation. *I should have stayed in the bloody car.*

He sighed dramatically. "Oh, you know how it is."

Yes, she knew. His wife didn't understand him and all that bollocks. Same old record. "So you haven't left her yet then?"

"No. She was diagnosed with cancer, so I'd be a bit of a bastard if I buggered off now, wouldn't I."

"If you don't feel the same about her then I'd say it was wicked to keep the relationship going." Maybe she should have been more compassionate, but her own problems took precedence—his were adding to her troubles.

He tugged on the dog's lead. "Pack it in with the jumping, Buddy. God, this dog's so pissing naughty." He shook his head. "So you think I should go anyway?"

"Does she know you're not happy and you're only staying with her because of how it would look to other people if you walked out?"

"No, I never did get around to telling her that things weren't right between us."

"Oh dear." What else was there to say? She wanted to tell him to sod off and leave her to walk in peace, but hadn't she been to see Father Donovan for a chat? Maybe her old client needed the same, for someone to listen. Did she have it in her today to be as kind as the priest? "Best to get it off your chest then."

She continued walking, and he followed, telling her all about it. It seemed he had similar feelings of guilt because he wished he'd left ages ago, before her diagnosis. Now he was stuck in a situation he didn't want to be in and felt bad that he wanted her to die already. Betty could relate; both of their thoughts weren't exactly classed as good ones.

"We all think things that other people wouldn't understand," she said. "Everyone must do it, it can't just be us. How long does she have left?"

"The doctor said about two years. Two fucking years, Widow. How am I going to stick around for that long?"

"Do you want to know my honest opinion?"

He nodded.

"Leave now, before you start to hate her and her last couple of years are miserable—it's not fair on her."

"But she's going to think it's because she got poorly."

"Not if you tell her how you've been feeling for God knows how long. You were seeing me for two years at the Bordello, and it was the same old story then. Why did you stay?"

"She earns more than me and pays all the bills. I had it easy and kept most of my wages to myself. If I left, I'd have had to pay out."

"Jesus Christ, that's honesty for you. But she'll have to give up her job at some point, so you'll have to pay out anyway."

"No, she's going to withdraw the pension she's been saving for years. As for honesty, I can talk to you, I've always been able to. You've never looked at me funny for telling the truth. You're actually the only person I *have* been able to speak to. When you left the Bordello I was gutted."

"Seems we've both got problems we're drowning in."

"What's up with you, then?"

She told him about Ezra, the brief highlights so he got the gist.

"Kick the little bastard out," he said. "There's no way I'd be putting up with him stealing from me, son or not. Actually, *because* he's your son it's even worse, and as for him calling you names… What you do for a living is more than just sex. Knowing I had someone to talk to every week kept me sane. You were more like my therapist."

She'd never looked at her profession in that way, but yes, she'd been a counsellor to many, an ear who listened. She wasn't just a slag.

"Do you want to come round mine once a week, Len?" she asked, then regretted it immediately. "Only to talk, mind, none of the other."

"Yeah, that would be lovely, but won't your kid be upset if he turns up and I'm there?"

"He doesn't live with me, and there's no chance in hell of him walking in on us." She gave him her address. "The Orange Lantern, have you heard of it? Listen, I need a bit of time on my own at the minute, but I'm not working tonight, so you could come round about eight. There's a side door I can let you in so you're not confused for a customer. I can make you a bit of dinner—as a *mate*—nothing fancy, maybe sausage and chips."

"I'll get it from the chippy on my way over. I don't like the thought of you waiting on me by cooking."

She gave him her phone number. Maybe having a friend to talk to other than Lainey would do her some good. She'd missed her since she'd moved out of that street. Texts and phone calls weren't the same as face-to-face natters.

She said her goodbyes and continued on round the lake alone, mulling over Len's situation and comparing it to hers. They were both in awful situations, but she conceded that maybe his was worse. As she didn't have many friends, barely anyone knew Ezra took drugs, whereas most of the people in Len's life would know his wife had cancer. If Betty refused to have anything to do with Ezra, there'd be no recriminations from anyone, as Lainey had told her months ago to kick him out of her life for good. Len, on the other hand, would have a lot of people having a go at him if he packed his bags.

She didn't bother with a second lap of the lake, instead heading towards her car, giving Father Donovan a wave as he said goodbye to one of his parishioners on the church steps. He waved back, and it felt nice to have an ally. In the car, she popped her seat belt on and drove away, pulling over two minutes later when an incoming call from the twins flashed up on the screen of her dashboard. Before she could talk herself out of it, she pressed ANSWER.

"Are you all right, Widow?" George asked.

"Not really, no. Did the priest get hold of you?"

"He did. Why didn't you ask for help sooner? We could have nipped his addiction in the bud ages ago."

"Leave it out, bruv," Greg said. "It sounds like you're making it her fault that he's still on drugs. Fucking think before you speak, will you?"

"Sorry," George said. "I didn't mean it to come out like that."

Widow smiled, relieved he wasn't angry at her for keeping this to herself. "It's okay, I'm glad I've got people on my side. Are you going to help me?"

"Yeah, what do you want us to do? Tell Cooper to pass it on to his runners that they're not to give your boy any drugs?"

"What's the point, he'd go elsewhere, and he's working for Cooper now anyway, so he has plenty of access to the fucking stuff."

"Fuck me sideways. Right, leave it with us to have a little think, and we'll get back to you when we've got a plan. First off, we'll put some men on surveillance to see what he's getting up to. Where does he live?"

"I don't know, it's a house with lads from college."

"It's fine. We'll get Cooper to find out for us."

"Won't he tell Ezra what's going on?"

"No, he knows better than to do that, but I'll reiterate to him that our discussion goes no further. He'd be a prick to go against us, considering we allow him to sell on Cardigan. You're not working tonight, are you, so go home and have a nice soak in the bath and try to forget about this for the evening."

"I've got a friend coming round. Actually, it's an ex-punter. We used to talk a lot when he came to see me at the Bordello. He's got his own problems, so we'll put the world to rights over dinner."

"Good for you, it's about time you thought less about work and your kid and more about yourself. Chat soon."

She drew up at the kerb outside the Lantern, and butterflies of anxiety flooded her chest. This was out of her hands now, and while she was glad she wasn't alone in this apart from having Lainey, she was worried about how the twins would handle Ezra. She homed in on George's comment about getting him off the drugs sooner, so it sounded like that was their intention. He hadn't been angry, like he wanted to teach Ezra some manners. But then if he did, would it be so bad? Her son had never had a male role model in his life, it had always been him and her, so a talking-to from a man might do the world of good, and the fact George was a Brother could only help matters, couldn't it?

She went indoors, the smell of fresh paint lingering from where the Lantern had been revamped to look more modern. She entered her attic apartment to have that soak George had suggested. In the warmth of the water, she let herself have a little cry: for the failure she'd been and how Ezra's prospects had turned to dust by one simple, wrong decision.

His decision, remember.

She'd never have thought this way before, that Ezra had to take some responsibility, but Father Donovan's words had penetrated. Yes, she'd always carry the guilt with her, but not all of it belonged to her. She'd see what happened when the twins intervened then go from there. Maybe they could bring the old Ezra back.

She got out of the bath and spent the next couple of hours wrapped in her dressing gown on the sofa with a blanket over her. She watched a film, thankfully losing herself in the plot and not thinking of her son once. He'd made his bed and would have to lie in it, but not for much longer, because the twins were going to yank him right out of it.

This was for the best. She had to believe that.

Chapter Four

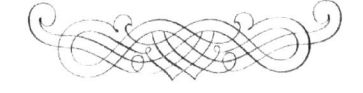

Ezra wasn't making enough money to cover his drug use. He thought by working for Cooper he would've been paid more, but that hadn't been the case. Stupid of him to have agreed to the job as a runner without discussing his wages first, but he'd been desperate. Mum was being funny about lending him money, and he could tell if he kept pushing her, she'd cut him off altogether. He'd already moved out because of the bad feeling between them, but he still visited her every week at the Orange Lantern, just to piss her off. Just to let her know he still called the shots regardless of The Brothers being her bosses.

Cooper had told him he ought to be careful where the twins were concerned, but as Ezra had never crossed their path, he doubted he ever would unless Mum grassed on him. She'd never do that, though. She was too uptight about being the same as her father—an arsehole. Ezra played that to his advantage, although sometimes, in the darkness of his room in the daytime, his blackout blind keeping the sun away, he thought about her when he couldn't sleep, and about himself and who he used to be—who he could have been now if he hadn't stepped off the good path.

Those times were the worst, full of recrimination and regret, those emotions exacerbated whenever the drugs slowly left his system. The core of him was still good, but the rest was absolutely fucked. He breezed around as if he didn't give a shit, and with heroin in his veins, he actually didn't. It was doing his head in, these swings-and-roundabout feelings. Thank God he'd stayed on track enough to pass his A levels, although what was the point of having them now if he wasn't going to uni or doing anything decent with his life?

He left his room and went down into the shared kitchen. One of his mates stood at the worktop buttering some toast.

"That job's tonight," Kash said, "so you'll have to call in sick or whatever it is you need to do."

Ezra had agreed to the job when he'd been high as a kite, and now he was on a downer, he wasn't sure he ought to do it. Yeah, it was a lot of money, and in an ideal world it would see him through with drugs for yonks, but he knew himself and he'd take more every day. Moving on from smoking heroin to injecting it had been one of his more stupid decisions, and chasing the dragon had become just that—he chased something he couldn't reach. Replicating that ultimate first high was unattainable. Now he shot up to take the feelings of craving away, the slicing claws in his stomach and the gnawing teeth on his nerves.

"Oh, right." Ezra flicked the kettle on. "It's still only me and you, yeah?"

Kash spluttered a laugh. "Any more than us two will draw attention. We'll be in and out in no time. I've borrowed my mate's van."

That meant it belonged to one of those blokes Ezra didn't like. They were loud and obnoxious, even more so than he was when he was doped up. He wasn't sure how heroin worked for other people, but as soon as it hit his veins, it was as if energy was zipped through him and he was invincible. But give him a couple of hours, and he was fucked out of his face, falling asleep. Should he inject before the job or would the adrenaline be enough to see him through?

"I don't think a lock pick is going to work there," he said.

"Well, that's where you're wrong because I tried it last night. Worked like a fucking charm."

"Did you go all the way in to check the shit's there?"

"Yeah, and it is. We're going to have to be quick, carry each one between us, put it in the van, then go back for another until we've got them all."

Ezra wasn't at his craving stage yet, so he was coherent enough to know that what they'd be stealing was wrong. The stuff was for prizes in a raffle tomorrow. He'd heard the twins had donated them, so when Kash had suggested they break in, Ezra had at first been excited about it, thanks to the rush of heroin, but out on the other side of it, he reckoned they were playing with fire. Even if they didn't get caught at the time, they could get caught later on. The twins weren't going to let the thieves get away with it, and they'd likely search for them until they were found. He didn't want to think about what they'd do to them after that.

"I'm not sure we should do this," he said. "Those twins—"

"—are not going to know it was us. Gloves, balaclavas, all that shit. We'll be sound."

What about the van number plate? What about CCTV?

He didn't bother saying that out loud. Kash would only shoot the worries down. Ezra made his coffee and sat at the table to roll a spliff. Kash fucked off somewhere with his toast, which was a bit of a relief. It'd be all right, wouldn't it? No one was ever around that area late at night, or so Kash had said, but as for being in and out in no time, even Ezra knew that wasn't possible. The goods they were stealing were bulky, and where they were stealing them from bothered him. It didn't sit right, but he'd committed to it now, so he'd get it over and done with, take the money from the sale of the items, and refuse to do any more jobs with Kash.

That's a lie and you know it.

That was the problem, he had the best intentions but never followed them through. Heroin had formed a new personality, mostly obliterating his old one. When he was high, he laughed at the person he used to be, the swot, the little nerd. At times he craved that person, though, wishing he could climb back into the old skin where he was safe and knew what tomorrow would bring. Sometimes the uncertainty of *this* life made him paranoid and he couldn't settle.

He glanced at his watch. Seven in the evening, what he classed as his morning because he worked overnight. Another four hours and they'd be starting the job. Maybe just a little injection wouldn't hurt. His muscles pinched, a warning that he needed a top-up soon. He worked out he'd be manic until nine and if he set an alarm, he could wake up at half ten, ready to get going.

He finished his spliff and coffee, deciding against using the needle. This was his issue, he couldn't fully settle on anything anymore, couldn't make a firm decision, his mind always flicking from one scenario to the other until it almost drove him mental.

Instead, he rolled another joint and added a small amount of heroin to it. That would have to do. Kash would go mad at him if he wasn't in any fit state to do the job, so it was best he smoke the hours away.

Before he forgot, he sent a message to Cooper.

EZRA: NOT GOING TO BE IN WORK THIS EVENING. STOMACH BUG.

COOPER: RIGHT.

He made another coffee and prepared to waste the next few hours.

※

They left the house on foot, hoods up, heads down, going around the corner to where Kash had left the van. They got in, Kash driving, and didn't speak for the whole journey, putting their gloves and balaclavas on after he'd parked. He opened the back doors so there was no fucking about when they bought the stuff out. They approached the large front door, Ezra struggling to walk properly—Kash had insisted on them putting heel lifts in too-big trainers so one, they looked taller to any witnesses, and two, if they left any footprints, their real sizes wouldn't match. Good job Ezra had pulled the laces tight and stuffed some tissue into the toes, otherwise he'd be tripping over.

He scoped the area to make sure they weren't being watched. Opposite, the park stood in darkness, and he squinted to try and make out any dog walkers or kids fucking about by the lake. Nothing. On this side of the street, an expanse of grass either side of the church, and then the cemetery beyond.

He turned back to face Kash who crouched and fiddled with the lock. Ezra had tamed his nerves with a fair few spliffs which had dulled his senses, although he hadn't dared tell Kash that. It took a lot of effort to concentrate, his head muggy, as though it was full of dense smoke. The lock clicked, and Kash pushed the door open enough that they could slip through. Inside, he closed it to, leaving enough of a gap that he could hook the toe of his boot around the edge and open it while their hands were full.

Mum had said she'd gone to church regularly before she'd had him, and he couldn't imagine her in a place like this, praying and shit. To either side, low lighting glowed, maybe plug-in lamps, which gave them enough light to see where they were going. Ezra followed Kash down the aisle, veering to the left into a corridor with two doors. Kash bent again and inserted the pick, the rattle of it loud and echoing, enough that Ezra got paranoid that the sound would filter outside. Not that anyone was likely to come by and hear it, but he still worried all the same.

"Got it," Kash whispered and stood to open the door.

With no light in here, Kash switched his phone torch on and flashed it around the room. Five large boxes containing seventy-inch flatscreen TVs. Seeing them reminded Ezra of a time he wasn't proud of, but he stuffed the guilt down.

"Come on, we need to get a move on," Kash said.

They took the first four out without any hassle, so Kash had been right that the job would be an easy one. Once they'd taken the fifth from the little room, Kash locked it so it'd look like an inside job and the priest would get the blame. He did the same with the front door, and they loaded the television into the van. Kash secured the doors and walked round to the driver's side as Ezra turned to walk the opposite way.

A man stood by the passenger door.

Ezra's brain struggled to work fast enough. He knew a bloke was there but he couldn't get his feet to move. Why did he have weird goggles on? Then something kicked in, the need to run, and he raced round the other side in the hope he could clamber over Kash in the driver's seat and they could get away, but the van pulled off, leaving Ezra on the pavement and the man in the road.

Ezra stared at him for a second then dashed towards the park, fear pulsing through him. Was that a random bloke or one of The Brothers' men? He pelted it over the grass, daring to look over his shoulder, convinced the man must be following him, but he remained on the road, staring Ezra's way. Scared, he kept running, through a patch of trees then out onto a housing estate, moving fast until he reached what he considered a safe place. He sat on a bench outside a row of shops and took the balaclava off, placing the gloves inside it and balling the lot up and putting it in his pocket.

It was then he caught up with the fact that Kash had abandoned him, and Mum's words came back to haunt him: *"People like that will drop you as soon as you're not useful anymore. Please stop hanging around with them."*

A few people came out of the pub along the way—there must have been a lock-in—laughing and talking, one of them shouting about what a fucking brilliant night they'd had. Ezra watched them for a while, imagining himself as part of their group, something that seemed so unattainable now, to be normal. Anger burned through him about Kash. Didn't he care whether that goggle bloke got hold of Ezra and marched him down the police station, or beat him up, or handed him over to the twins?

So long as he got away with the tellies, he doesn't give a fuck.

Ezra stood and began the walk back to his house, contemplating a detour to the Lantern along the way, telling Mum what had happened and asking for help, but why bother, she'd only be at work with the pervs, or she'd tell him he shouldn't have gone out robbing in the first place.

At the end of his street, he stood by a bush to check for anyone who shouldn't be out at this time. The van wasn't in sight, so Kash was probably returning it to his mate after dropping off the TVs to the fella who wanted them nicked. What if he didn't give Ezra his share of the dosh? What if he said he'd only done half the job so he wasn't getting paid? It wasn't like Ezra was strong enough to have a fight with him over it. Kash would always win.

He continued to the next street along and dipped down an alley. He went indoors via the back garden. The house had that empty feel, but he went upstairs to Kash's room anyway to see if he was home. He wasn't, and Ezra checked his watch then pulled his phone out.

EZRA: I'M FEELING BETTER NOW, SO CAN I COME INTO WORK?

COOPER: FILLED YOUR SPACE. COME TOMORROW.

There was nothing for Ezra to do but sit and wait for Kash to come back.

Who was that man in the road? Now they'd been seen outside the church, the plan for the priest to be accused of the theft might not hold water, unless a rumour went round that he'd hired two men in balaclavas and given them the keys. Something niggled at the back of Ezra's mind, a warning that he shouldn't have gone on that job tonight. He'd had the same thing earlier, hadn't he, and had stupidly still gone along with it.

He toyed with his phone, wavering on whether to send Mum a message or not. What would he even say? That he wanted to come home? That he was sorry for everything he'd done? How could he go home, though, when she'd moved out of the only place of safety he knew? She lived in that sex house now amongst all those slags.

By the time he'd shot heroin into his veins, he had no such compulsion to make contact. Fuck her.

Chapter Five

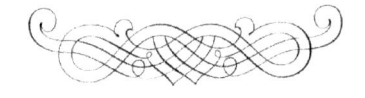

"I need two hundred quid because I owe this lad an' that..." Sometimes, Ezra hated keep asking his mum for money, but who else was he supposed to turn to? He had no clue who his dad was, he could be one of God knows how many, and who was to say the bloke was a decent enough person to help his son out anyway?

"What did you borrow two hundred pounds for?" Mum eyed him funny from where she stood at the sink washing up a griddle pan.

"Weed."

"And what makes you think I'm prepared to pay for that?"

"Because if you don't, the lad'll come round here for the money. He'll give you a clout an' shit, a black eye."

"Then I'd phone the police."

"Nah, you don't want to be doing that, not with this bloke. He's got this friend, and they both go round in masks and sunglasses. People get sliced up, d'you know what I mean?"

She hated his way of talking, she'd said so often enough, and the kid he used to be would have stopped it straight away (actually, he wouldn't have even started it in the first place), but the kid he was now did it even more to annoy her. Maybe it was hormones, but he felt itchy on the inside, as if his skin didn't fit him properly. The only thing that made him feel better was smoking a spliff, but lately that had progressed from it just being your average blunt to having certain extras sprinkled into it before he rolled it up.

It seemed heroin got a damn good grip on you, and if he didn't get his fix, he took it out on others. He didn't want to have to do that to his mum; despite him *calling her a slag and giving her grief, he still loved her. She'd bought him up all on her own, and he owed her everything, so why was he such a cunt to her? Why didn't he take the help she'd offered countless times, where she'd send him somewhere so he could get off the drugs?*

"Yes, I know exactly what you mean," she said.

It sounded like she was referring to Roach and Boycie, like she knew them or something, which wasn't even possible. All right, he'd mentioned their names, but there was no way she could know them.

"So are you going to give it to me then or what?" he asked.

"If you clean this house for me while I'm at work, then yes, you can have it, but not until then."

"Are you fucking kidding me?"

"No, I want to see a clean house before I hand over any money. Cash doesn't come for free, and it's about time you realised that. If you want to earn two hundred a week as my cleaner, be my guest."

She'd started a new job but hadn't told him where it was. At one time he'd have asked her out of curiosity, but to be honest, he didn't really give a fuck so long as she wasn't at that Bordello place. Whatever she was doing made her more money than before, because usually when he asked for cash she said she was strapped, whereas now she had it to hand. He supposed she was trying to teach him the value of money and that you had to work for it, but he wasn't interested in any of that shit. Work was for pricks. So long as he had a roof over his head, then he had nothing to worry about.

"All right then." He was that desperate for some more drugs that he'd do what she wanted. He owed Roach's runner one hundred, so that would give him another hundred to buy some more.

Mum stared at him. "What? No arguing?"

"I CBA."

"I don't even know what that means, Ezra."

"I can't be arsed."

"What, to tell me what it means?"

He wanted to punch the wall. Why was she so thick? "No, it means I can't be arsed. CBA, get it? Fucking hell." He slouched out of the kitchen and went upstairs. Better to start cleaning up there while she was still in the house, otherwise she'd spy on him to see if he was doing it right.

Ten minutes later she called up him, "Send me pictures of a nice sparkling house and then I'll pop the money in your bank account."

"Whatever," he shouted back.

He stood to the side of her bedroom window and watched her get into her new car. It wasn't new-new, she wasn't earning that much as far as he knew, but it was new to her. He hadn't even known she could drive, and when he'd asked her, she'd said his granddad had paid for her lessons and test before he'd found out she was pregnant. He must have been a nice bloke deep down to have done that, but then what kind of bastard chucked a kid out just because they were up the duff? Ezra didn't want to know the man or his wife. The pair of them had left Mum to cope by herself, so as far as he was concerned, they were dead to him.

His mother drove away, and she seemed so proud of herself to have been able to afford the car. Sometimes he felt such a monster for treating her the way he did, but then when he needed the drugs, he turned into a different person. He wished he'd never started smoking weed, wished the kids at college had never come up to him and made friends. He should have stuck with being a geek but, desperate to fit in, he'd grabbed the chance to belong to something he'd only ever watched from the sidelines at school: a group of lads mucking about; in-jokes; people who had your back.

When they'd first taken him to meet the runner, he hadn't had a clue what was happening. He'd never seen a drug deal go down before, so when one of them had shaken hands with the runner, he'd thought they were being matey. It wasn't until later and the kid had shown him what was in his hand that Ezra had twigged what had gone on.

It was at that point he should have walked away, but he hadn't, and now he was doing secret handshakes with the runner himself. It was so obvious now, to see how it happened, how the drug business expanded: a mate brought along a mate who brought along a mate...

When he got the balls up, he was going to ask Roach if he could work for him, then he wouldn't have to ask Mum for any money, but it might mean getting off the gear. He'd heard Roach didn't employ anyone who sniffed, smoked, or injected.

While he was in Mum's room, he had a root around in case she'd hidden any cash anywhere, but knowing her, she would have bought a little safe to keep it in. There wasn't one under the bed or in the back of the wardrobe, and he even nosed in the airing cupboard in case she'd put it behind the sheets, pillowcases, and towels.

Maybe her job paid into the bank. Maybe it was a legitimate one where she didn't take notes from the grubby hands of perverted customers. It was about time she got herself off that merry-go-round, the dirty cow.

He got caught up in searching the whole house for hidey-holes where money could be, and by the time he'd finished, he'd made a bit of a mess. He set about putting everything back from where he taken it, then after that he did the actual cleaning. It took him two hours. Because of his massive itch to get some more gear in his bloodstream, he'd paid proper attention when scrubbing the bathroom, using a toothbrush round the bases of the taps and everything. He took photos for her and sent them over WhatsApp, and she responded that the cash was in his account.

He stalked out of the house, checking his bank app as he walked along the street. He stank of lemon spray cleaner but was too twitchy to give much of a shit. He went through the park and out onto the street where the runner worked.

"You'd best have my hundred quid," the kid said. "I trusted you and had to use my own money to hand over the takings to Roach. You're two days late, and my kid needs some formula."

Ezra closed his eyes. "Fuck, my old dear put it in the bank." He got his phone out to show him his account. "See, I've got it."

"It's cash, bruh, you know that. Go to the fucking machine and come back."

Ezra had no choice but to run across the grass behind the runner and into the trees. He weaved between trunks, coming out on a curving street that would lead to a parade of shops. With his head down and his muscles flickering all over, he walked past the Chinese and the little Tesco, then waited in the two-person queue at the cashpoint.

It was then he realised he hadn't brought his bank card. He stormed home, and by the time he got back to the cashpoint and then the runner, another hour had gone by and he was tweaking like a motherfucker. He handed the two hundred over, snatched his drugs, and tromped across the grass to sit on the bench near the tree line. Everyone around here knew this bench belonged to the druggies, and he was ashamed of himself for having to sit on it. Once upon a time he'd walked down this street and glanced over, shaking his head at how dumb the two kids were who'd sat there shooting up. And now he was one of those kids, hooked and floundering one minute, hooked and indestructible the next.

He prepared his smoke and toked on it, the good shit entering his bloodstream, making him feel better almost instantly. He stared at the night sky, the hint of lemon scent hanging around him. He'd forgotten to eat today. He finished his joint and slouched off to the parade of shops, ordering chips and curry sauce at the Chinese. He sat on a stone seat next to the rubbish bins to eat it, feeling all right now, less wobbly and more in control.

He used to feel like that all the time before he'd started taking drugs, but now he had to put what amounted to poison in his body in order to feel human, and even then, that didn't last long because he got tired and tended to nod off.

Belly full, he went home for a kip, only to find Roach getting out of a car in front of the house. Ezra's legs almost gave way, but he acted nonchalant and continued down the pavement as if he wasn't scared.

In his mask and sunglasses, with Boycie standing beside him blocking the path, Roach said, "I hear you had some stuff on tick."

"I paid it back."

"Yeah, I know, but you were two days late. Do you need my mate here to slit your throat in order for you to understand that we're not messing? There are rules, and if you're told a certain time to pay something back, you fucking pay it back."

"I won't borrow drugs again. I swear down, I'll wait until I've got the money before I buy any."

Roach nodded, ominous-looking with his hood up. "I don't like having to come out to talk to people. There are enough rumours going around about me that people tend to do as they're told without me having to make an appearance. I haven't built up my reputation this long for someone like you to come along and flout the rules. Did you think my runner was fucking joking when he said you had a certain amount of time to pay it back? Did you think he was talking for the sake of it?"

"Nah, it's just I don't want to have to ask my mum for the money again because I keep asking and she keeps giving it to me."

"That's another thing. You'd better watch how you treat her. She works for me now."

Ezra couldn't comprehend that. "Um, what?"

"You heard me."

"She's selling drugs? Nah, there's no way she'd do that. No fucking way."

"She isn't, but what she is *doing pays for your dirty little habit, so you remember in future, whenever you want to give her a bit of backchat, that without her you wouldn't be able to buy the drugs in the first place. Have a bit of respect. If I find out you've fucked her about, I'll be back."*

Roach and Boycie got in the car, driving away slowly, Roach holding up two fingers, miming holding a gun. Ezra pissed himself, hot liquid trickling down one leg and into his trainer. Scared, confused, and ashamed, he went inside, shoving his clothes and trainers in the washing machine, then going to have a shower. For the first time in a long while, he planned to stay in all night, not just have a quick kip and then go out to meet his friends. He reckoned he was better off keeping his head down for the time being.

He hid his stash under the carpet in the corner and got in bed, wishing he didn't find himself crying into his pillow because of the stupid decisions he'd made.

Chapter Six

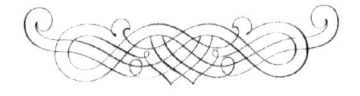

Jason Ludlow still stood in the street outside the church, unsure what to do. He never thought he'd actually *see* anybody up to no good, so it had been a bit of a shock. He came here every evening to keep an eye out. He loved Our Lady, her beautiful bricks and stained-glass windows, and her bell tower, although when the bells rung, his head buzzed.

When those two men had come along in their van, he'd watched from his bench by the lake in the darkness of the park, his night-vision goggles on, the ones Gran had bought him. He'd thought maybe the people were delivering something and Father Donovan would be along any moment, but they had a key. That had puzzled him, but he'd convinced himself that the priest had given it to them. Then they'd come out with those big telly boxes, and he'd hovered his thumb over the number nine on the keypad of his phone, wanting to ring the police but stopping himself in case Father Donovan had arranged for these men to collect them.

They were supposed to be for the fayre tomorrow.

In this situation, he didn't know what to do for the best or what was right. Normally that wouldn't be a problem, because he knew what was right and wrong. Tonight, though, the telly removal could be right, but on the other hand, it could be very wrong. Panic had risen inside him, butterflies fluttering, and he'd switched to his contact list to find Father Donovan's number instead.

But then the last box had been carried out, and they'd locked the church door. Jason had lumbered over the grass, wanting to ask them what they were doing, but courage had deserted him and he'd stared at the man who'd then run away.

Why had he run? Jason didn't think he looked scary in his goggles, but Gran said he was tall and wide, so maybe that was it. Other people called him a retard. That word wasn't supposed to be spoken anymore, but the bullies didn't care. They thought they were allowed to do whatever they liked.

Now he stood on the steps of Our Lady, thinking maybe the man would come back, and so would the one in the van so he could pick his mate up. Jason reckoned those two had been well sensible to wear balaclavas and gloves tonight. It was really cold, and he wished he hadn't left his bobble hat and mittens behind with Gran. He slapped his palms together to generate some warmth—the tips of his fingers had gone numb—and stamped his feet, his breaths coming out as little grey clouds.

He waited for quite a while, losing track of time, but the man or the van didn't come back. Maybe the driver had collected him elsewhere.

Jason glanced at the glowing blue face of his watch. Oh God. Gran was going to tell him off because he was late. She might not be too mad, though, because there were no texts or missed phone calls from her—she was maybe doing what she'd said and letting him have more leeway. He made his way home, finding her waiting at the front door with her hands on her hips. She'd have been watching for him from her chair by the window and got up to let him in.

"What have I told you?" she whispered. "There are lots of nasty people out there, and you know you have to be home by eleven."

"I was going to come home when a van pulled up outside Our Lady."

She tutted and glanced up and down the street. "Keep your voice down, the neighbours are asleep. What do you mean, a van?"

She retreated inside, and Jason followed, relieved to be able to tell someone about what he'd seen. He still had some butterflies floating in his tummy, and it was uncomfortable. He felt like *he'd* done something wrong, and he supposed he had if you counted the fact he was home late.

He shut the door, put the chain on, and took his coat off, hanging it on the newel post. He told Gran all about what he'd seen, and she leaned against the living room doorframe, her arms folded and her bottom lip between her teeth.

"And they saw you," she said. "Two men in balaclavas saw you watching them."

He couldn't work out if she was angry or not. "They didn't know I watched them take the tellies, just that I was at the van when they went to get in."

"Well, I think you'll be all right. It sounds like that man ran away because he was scared, and the same goes for the other one driving off. They saw a big bloke like you and shit themselves."

Normally, she would have told him that the balaclava men might come back for him tomorrow night, or any of the other nights he kept watch at Our Lady, so if she hadn't said that, then she *must* think everything would be okay. He didn't think she'd keep something that important to herself.

"I don't want you going back there," she said.

And he worked out that she'd said it after all, she'd just used different words. She was funny like that, his Gran; sometimes she didn't outright state things like he needed her to, but for the most part, he'd learned how to read what she meant. At times, though, he got it really wrong, and she got cross but then said sorry afterwards because it wasn't his fault.

Jason was thirty now, not thirteen, and Gran had to understand that adults were allowed to make their own decisions. "I'll stay in the park like you told me to. I like looking after the church, and I don't want anyone scaring me away."

"Make sure you do that then. You can use your goggles from beside the lake. There's no need for you to go up close." She patted his arm. "A cup of tea before bed then."

Jason nodded and followed her into the kitchen.

Chapter Seven

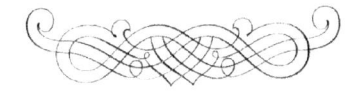

Father Michael Donovan listened to Kathleen Ludlow's voice coming out of his speakerphone, and his heart sank. He was well aware that Jason stood in the park every evening, watching his precious church, but he never thought he'd actually see something happening there. A part of him wondered whether Jason had been the one to tell the men where the televisions were. He hung around at the church a lot, watching and listening, and until now, Michael hadn't thought anything of it, except that Jason needed something to occupy his days. His obsession with all things to do with Our Lady was highly apparent, but as he was doing no harm, Michael had allowed it to continue.

Ashamed of his thoughts regarding Jason possibly passing on information he shouldn't have, Michael thanked Kathleen for letting him know about the robbery and asked her to keep it to herself.

"Because you're in with The Brothers now, aren't you?" she said.

Michael rolled his eyes—another thing Jason had picked up on. *More fool me for thinking he wasn't taking any notice of who popped in to see me.* "Yes, they've been a blessing for the church, as well as St Thomas'. Their donations are appreciated."

"I expect the amount of money they must have, they'll be able to replace those tellies without blinking an eye."

"But they shouldn't have to, Kathleen. Those men shouldn't have stolen them in the first place, but thank goodness for Jason, otherwise we'd never have known how many men we were dealing with."

"He's going to think he's James Bond now, you know that, don't you. He'll want to find who did it, and it could put him in danger. I worry about his decision-making and where it'll lead him."

Personally, Michael thought she coddled Jason too much. The man was cannier than he was given credit for, although he'd concede that if approached by thugs, Jason wouldn't know how to respond. He might be big and strong, but he didn't have a violent bone in his body.

"I'll tell him I'd rather he watch from the park," Michael said. "I'll say God would want him to keep out of the way, which He would."

"That should do it. Well, I shall certainly keep this to myself, and it's time I was in bed. Jason can't be that worried because I can hear him snoring through the ceiling."

"Good, I'd hate to think of him being upset and unable to sleep."

Michael said goodbye and ended the call. In normal circumstances he would have telephoned the police to inform them of the robbery, but he was fully aware he'd entered a different arena now, where the rules were slightly different. He glanced at the clock, super conscious of the time, but George had told him that if anything was wrong, he must contact them no matter what.

He pressed the icon to connect their call and held his breath for a moment.

"Everything all right, Vicar?" George asked.

Michael didn't correct him to say he preferred the term priest; he sensed George would call him a vicar even more if he did. "I'm afraid it's bad news. Two men came and stole the televisions."

"I beg your fucking pardon?"

Michael took that as an outburst of shock, so he didn't bother repeating what he'd said. "One of my parishioners, Jason Ludlow, saw them arrive in a white Transit around eleven p.m. They had balaclavas on and a key to the church door. I assume that was a lock pick, as I certainly don't leave my keys lying around for anyone to take them away to get copies. Jason said one of them ran away and the other drove off when they saw him. I suspect they were scared, as Jason is quite tall and imposing."

"What did you do, ask him to watch the church while the televisions were in there?"

"No, Jason has taken it upon himself to watch the church every night. He has done for the past four years. During the day, he spends his time inside, talking to other parishioners, tidying the Bibles, that sort of thing."

"Hasn't he got a fucking job, or is he some weirdo who likes hanging around religious places?"

"He's neurodiverse, that's as much as I know."

"Oh, now I feel a bastard…"

"He lives with his gran because his mother gave him up when she realised he wasn't the perfect little boy she wanted."

"Well, that's fucking cuntish on her part," George said. "What's her name? I'd like to have a word with her."

"I have no idea. The gran, Kathleen, has never mentioned it and I've never asked. I prefer to let members of the flock come to me of their own accord, rather than me force them into confessing anything. Now before I say what I have to say, please remember Jason can't help some of the things he does. As he's in the church most of the time—and I'm not joking there, he brings a packed lunch—he would have known where the televisions were stored. He has an innocence about him where he thinks everybody's as pure as he is, so if he mentioned the televisions or where they were, it wouldn't have been with any malice or to encourage someone to steal them. He'd have probably said how exciting it was to have them in the raffle. He wouldn't have thought anybody would have wanted to take them away."

"Poor bastard. We'll leave him alone because we don't want to be upsetting him. Can you let him know if he did say anything, it's not his fault? It's the wankers who took the tellies—they made that decision, not him."

"I shan't put it quite that way with such colourful language, but yes, I'll explain it to him. In future, if anything needs to be kept quiet, I'm going to have to tell him outright that he mustn't speak about it." Michael sighed. "But I don't want to get into the habit of asking him to keep secrets."

"It's either that or turf him out of your church, mate. If he's going to be a liability, and if our donations are going to end up being pinched… Then again, we can store them until the day of any fayres. And seeing as the leaflets have all been sent out announcing televisions are prizes, then we're going to have to replace them."

"That's very kind of you, and I didn't doubt you for a second on that score."

"It goes without saying that you need to keep your eyes and ears open now. We'll find out who did this between us."

Michael had expected as much. After all, he'd stepped into the lion's den willingly, and doing his part was what he'd agreed to. It wouldn't look odd, him asking questions. It was nothing he wouldn't have done had the twins not been involved with Our Lady. Perhaps their involvement was to Michael's advantage. People were more likely to talk if they knew they might be in trouble with George or Greg if they kept something a secret.

The questioning would have to wait until the morning, though. For now he had to drive to the church and ensure it was actually locked. Kathleen had said Jason observed the men securing the door, but Michael wouldn't trust anyone who'd said that. Our Lady was too important to him to not go there and at least check.

The drive there didn't take long, and he sat parked at the kerb for a while, peering into the blackness of the park and also at the trees either side of the church. For the first time, he felt afraid of being here; anyone could be lurking. He took a deep breath and removed the keys from his pocket, then got out of his car. He hurried to the front door and shoved the big key in, twisting it quickly and going inside. The glow of the night lights gave him comfort.

Should he lock himself in, just in case those men came back? But what if they were inside again, coming in undetected because Jason had gone home? If Michael needed to run, he'd be hampered by having to unlock the door.

"Is anyone here?" he called—stupid of him, because it wasn't like a robber would respond.

He made up his mind and locked the door, hastening down the aisle and going straight to the room where the televisions had been stored. He tried the handle; the door was locked, so those men had most definitely used a pick. He slid the key in and went inside, flicking the light on, shaking his head at the absence of the television boxes. Nothing else had been taken—not the boxes of plastic cups and cutlery, the paper plates, the stacks and stacks of pop in cases, the crisps and cakes. The sandwiches were being delivered tomorrow, as where the sausage rolls and pork pies, the freshly baked scones, butter, jam, and clotted cream to go with them. The twins had organised everything. They'd taken the stress out of what was usually a situation fraught with apprehension. It was such a shame that it had been tainted by the theft.

He exited and locked the door, checking the rest of the church for any intruders. He left the bell tower until last, climbing the many steps, pausing on the halfway landing to stare out at the street. His stomach rolled over. A man sat in a car beneath a lamppost, staring straight up at Michael. The fella lifted a hand and stuck his thumb up as if to convey he was no threat.

Michael took his phone out of his pocket and accessed his messages. He'd turned all sounds off bar for calls earlier so hadn't heard anything coming in.

GG: SURVEILLANCE OUTSIDE THE CHURCH FROM NOW ON, DONE IN SHIFTS. BLUE FORD FIESTA.

MICHAEL: I'M AT THE CHURCH NOW. I SEE IT.

GG: WHAT THE FUCK ARE YOU DOING THERE?

MICHAEL: I WANTED TO MAKE SURE THE PLACE WAS LOCKED. EVERYTHING ELSE IN THE STOREROOM IS STILL THERE, SO I CAN ONLY ASSUME THEY DIDN'T WANT TO STAY HERE FOR LONG ENOUGH TO CLEAR THE WHOLE ROOM OUT.

GG: SOUNDS TO ME LIKE THE TELLIES WERE THE TARGET AND NOTHING MORE. GO HOME AND GET SOME SLEEP. IT'S A BUSY DAY TOMORROW.

MICHAEL: OKAY. GOODNIGHT.

He slid his phone in his pocket and continued up the stairs. Finding no one in the bell-ringing room, he made his way back down and left the church, locking up then getting in his car. He'd have to get the locks changed tomorrow to the kind where picks would be useless.

He stared across at the man in the Ford, memorising his face, then drove off towards home. He didn't think he'd sleep much tonight, and he didn't relish the prospect of talking to Jason tomorrow, trying to explain things in a way he would understand.

Sometimes, being a priest was hard work.

Chapter Eight

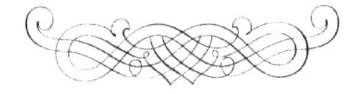

Two o'clock in the morning wasn't exactly the greatest time to drop in on someone, but when George had a bee in his bonnet about something, he didn't give a fuck *what* time it was. Widow was going to have to shut the fuck up if she had an opinion on him and Greg turning up on her night off—and besides, she wanted their help, so any grumbles she had could be parked right up her arse.

With regards to finding out if Jason Ludlow had a criminal record, their hands were tied for now, as neither of their inside police officers were on shift at the minute. DS Colin Broadly had been staying with their ex-copper, Janine, and her boyfriend, Cameron, because he had a knack of settling their baby daughter, Rosie. Since she'd gone into a proper sleeping pattern, he was back at home now, finding it lonely there since his wife's rape and murder. As for Anaisha Bolton, she wasn't exactly in the right department at the station to be able to help them most of the time, but she was good for using other officers' details to log in and access certain information.

It was probably as Father Donovan had said, that Jason had unwittingly passed on information or someone overheard him talking about the televisions. As he spent the majority of his day at the church, that meant the thieves were possibly churchgoers themselves—hardly the types of people who should be into stealing, but many a Catholic or Christian hid sins beneath their skin, sweetness and light on the outside, the Devil himself inside.

However, if it wasn't anything to do with Jason, then there was a possible leak in the twins' firm, or maybe even the bloke who'd sold the tellies from a family business in town had got it into his head to nick them back. They'd be going to Currys in the morning to get replacements.

"They had to have known that we bought the TVs," George said.

"I wondered when you were going to pipe up." Greg took a left turn. "Not necessarily. Not everyone has their ear to the ground or even gives a shit we exist—sorry if that upsets your ego. They could have assumed the TVs were donated by other people. But if they did know we bought them and chose to steal them anyway, then they've got some balls on them, don't you think? Considering the consequences…"

"Or their need for the televisions was greater than any fear they had for us."

"Like Widow's kid."

"Exactly."

Their man outside Ezra's house said two young men left the property earlier and walked down the street, but by the time he'd got the engine started and followed, they were gone.

George sighed. "They're too tall to be Ezra, though."

"Good job I'd already guessed where your mind had wandered to, otherwise I wouldn't have known what you were on about. So they're possibly two of the blokes he lives with. Bennett didn't catch any sightings of the van on CCTV, so we're shit out of luck there."

"That's because the route from their house to the church hasn't got any cameras." George was getting arsier by the second.

"Why did you even want to come and see Widow, and why couldn't it wait until the morning?"

"Because I'm pissed off that two scrotes nicked our tellies, and I want to find out whether Ezra's the type to happily land his friends in it if he thought he was in trouble with us."

"He sounds like he'll do anything for a bit of cash, so he might well dob them in, but this is nothing a simple text message wouldn't have sorted out."

"You know what I'm like, I prefer to feel like I'm *doing* something. I get ants in my pants."

"Yeah, well, I wish they'd fuck off because I'm ready for my bed."

"Shut up moaning."

Greg pulled up to the kerb. Out of the taxi, they walked up the path towards the Lantern. A quick tap on the door, and one of their security guards answered. He'd seen George and Greg in their myriad wigs and beards before, so he nodded and let them in, closing the door behind them.

"I assume Widow's up in her flat," George said. "Or her apartment, as she likes to call it."

"Yeah, she said she didn't want to be disturbed once her mate turned up." The guard stressed the word *mate* so must have thought Widow was entertaining this evening in more ways than one.

"It is actually just a mate," George said, "and even if it wasn't, less of the insinuation and judging. What she does with her own life is her business."

"Sorry."

"So you should be."

George led the way upstairs, and on the landing, he pressed the bell on the door to Widow's place. The tap of her feet on the stairs came, then she opened up, frowning.

"Oh God, what's happened?"

"We don't think your lad was involved, so don't panic, but he might have known about it. Can we come up for a chat?"

She snorted. "We both know that wasn't a request."

She turned and went up the stairs, opening another door at the top. "Known about what? What's going on?"

George ignored her and entered the living room, immediately zeroing in on a bloke sitting on her sofa—older than her by a mile with the air of a punter about him. Maybe she *was* making some money on the side to top up her ever-depleting pot because her shit of a son kept sponging off her.

"All right," George said to him by way of greeting.

The bloke shook and jumped to his feet, sticking his hand out. "My name's Len Smith and I live at fifteen Baldry Close. I'm married and I've got a dog called Buddy and a goldfish called Scales. I'm an accountant and drive a Volkswagen Golf."

George gripped his hand firmly, just to shit him up, even though he was suitably shitted up already. "I don't need your life story, but nice to meet you. Sit your arse down before you fall down with fright. We're honestly not that bad — so long as you toe the line."

Len lowered back to the sofa, casting a quick glance at Widow. "Fucking hell," he whispered to her. "I've just gone and made the biggest dickhead of myself, haven't I?"

She laughed. "Unfortunately, yes. And even more unfortunately, George probably won't let you forget it." She sat beside him and looked up at George. "Come on then, what's happened?"

George sat on the other sofa beside Greg who'd already made himself at home. "Cooper let us know where your boy lives, and we've had surveillance round there all evening. Two lads in black clothing left the house, both about five-nine. Now I know that can't be Ezra, because you said he's five-six, so they're more than likely two of the fellas he lives with. Our man didn't get a proper look at them because they bent their heads, and by the time he got going to follow them round the corner, they were gone. According to en eye witness, a few minutes later, two men in balaclavas got out of a Transit and entered Our Lady of St Patrick's, possibly using a lock pick. They stole five seventy-inch flatscreen televisions that we'd bought for the church raffle tomorrow."

"Shit. It'll be for drugs. I bet the lot of them are in on it." Widow pressed the pads of her index fingers against each temple. "I feel responsible just because my son knows them—if it's the same blokes."

"Their actions aren't your problem," Len said, taking one of her hands and holding it in his lap. "We've already talked about this tonight. You've done your best with that boy, and he chose to throw it back in your face."

"I agree," Greg said. "The reason we're here is because we haven't been able to get any background on Ezra as such, only what you've told us. We need to know whether he's the type to grass his mates up if we offer him cash for information."

"I'd like to say no," Widow said, "but I'd be lying. He'd sell anyone down the river these days if it meant having money in his pocket."

"I think we ought to go around there now," George said. "Break into their fucking house and pull them out of their beds, get them talking."

"I'm playing devil's advocate here, but could it be a coincidence?" Len asked. "Loads of kids wear all black, and they could have gone round the corner to a mate's house. They might not know anything about a van or any tellies."

"Then they've got nothing to worry about when it comes to answering our questions, have they?" Now George had got it inside his head, he wanted to leave and get round to that bastard house. Just imagining yanking lads off their mattresses had his adrenaline pumping. "Right, we'll be off then." He stood and looked down at Len. "Do you need a lift or are you staying the night?"

"I was about to go when you arrived. I've got my own car, thanks. I can't leave Buddy with the wife all night. She wouldn't let him out for his usual wee at four."

George shrugged. "We'll see ourselves out."

He tromped downstairs and out to the taxi. In the passenger seat, he stuck his safety belt on and waited for Greg to get in. "If we get them out of their beds, they might be disorientated enough to spill the beans."

"Or the night-time could be their daytime and they're high as anything. I suppose that could help get them talking an' all." Greg started the engine and drove towards Ezra's place. "That Len was a bit of a scaredy cat, wasn't he?"

"Some people go a bit funny when they meet us. God knows why." George grinned. "Poor fucker. I'm surprised he didn't piss his pants." He sniffed. "I know I basically told the security guard to mind his own business, but d'you reckon she's seeing Len on the side?"

"Fuck knows, but she deserves some happiness. You know when she said she took the job at the Lantern so she could kill Roach? I wonder what stopped her from doing it?"

"Maybe she had an attack of conscience. She might have got so caught up with Ezra's bollocks that she forgot Roach was the cause of it all in a way."

"People have a choice when they're first presented with whether to take a drug. Ezra made his. Whether Roach was the supplier or not, I expect Ezra would have ended up taking them anyway because he was hanging around with a bad element."

"Still is if his mates nicked the tellies."

Greg waved a hand. "Shut up now. We're here. We don't need the neighbours waking up."

They got out of the taxi, George striding towards the front door. He used a lock pick, which proved tricky at first, but then they were in. There was a distinct smell of weed in the air but no sign of lingering smoke as the light was off in the hallway. George glanced upstairs, and that was in darkness, too, but downstairs to the right, a slice of yellow light at the bottom of a door, mellow music filtering beneath it. He supposed they were smoking weed and chilling out.

Quietly, he moved towards the kitchen at the back, also in darkness, turning to the right and peering at silhouettes. A small table and chair set had been moved to block the back door, and where they might have stood prior to that in the centre of the dining area, the obvious shape of boxes stood out.

Taking a moment to compose himself so he didn't go off on one, George took his phone out and used the torch app, shining the beam at the boxes. Their fucking television boxes. Torch off, he returned to Greg by the front door and whispered about his find.

"Did you bring a gun?" Greg asked.

"I did as it happens."

"Then you might need to get it out, because if there's more than two people in that living room, we'll need a shooter to persuade them to do as they're told. Either that or we wait for backup. There's the chance they'll have guns themselves if they think they're little gangsters."

George took his gun out of the holster, tapped his bulletproof vest to remind himself he had one on, and held up a finger to tell Greg he wanted him to stay where he was. "In case they try to escape," he said quietly. In reality, he'd rather the pricks shot him than Greg.

He twisted the handle and opened the door about an inch. There wasn't enough of a gap yet to peer through the space by the hinges, so he looked at the view on the other side. A slice of television with some music video playing. A curtain billowed, so the window had been opened since they'd come inside. A cold draught from the December air wafted towards George along with the scent of marijuana. He pushed the door a little more, gun clenched tight, then he shoved it wide and jumped into the room, weapon raised.

Four lads lounged on sofas at the back behind a haze of drug mist. Their delayed reactions afforded George enough time to study their faces, and going by Widow's description, Ezra was the kid crapping himself closest to the right-hand corner. He hugged his bare torso, sweat breaking out on his forehead. Fear? No one reached for a weapon, they stared in stupefied silence, so for the most part they must be so off their faces that they didn't understand how much shit they were in.

"Who went to Our Lady of St Patrick's tonight?" George asked.

No one responded.

One of them did his sweatshirt up and drew the hood over his head.

"If you weren't smoking that shit, you wouldn't have had to open the window, and then you wouldn't be cold, would you?" George said. "So no one's going to answer my question, then?"

He stared at each of them in turn. Only Ezra's expression leaned towards guilt, but that could be because he'd been a good lad at one time and his morals were still there, just buried too deep. Or he could be the type who looked guilty even when he was innocent.

"Stand up," he ordered.

All four got to their feet.

"I'm George Wilkes, by the way, one of The Brothers, but I expect you've gathered that by now."

"Didn't know you were ginger and had a beard," one of them said on a giggle.

"There's a lot of things you don't know, sunshine, like how, when I find out who went to Our Lady earlier, I'm going to fuck them the fuck up."

Mr Chatty Man paled and held both hands up. "It wasn't me, I swear."

"We don't even know what you're on about," another one said.

George smiled. "What about you, Ezra? Do *you* know anything?"

The kid blanched, clearly shocked at George knowing his name, but if he'd been paying attention, he'd have known his mother now worked for them.

"Someone must know," George went on, "because I've seen the fucking television boxes out there in the kitchen. They didn't appear there all by themselves, did they. Now then, two of you were seen leaving this house before the tellies got robbed. I'm suggesting you got into a Transit around the corner, went to the church, and stole the televisions." He pointed to the two tallest who matched the heights their surveillance man had mentioned. "So you pair are coming with us."

"What?" one of them shouted.

"Does smoking joints make you deaf?" George asked. "My mum used to say it affected people in different ways, so I'll say it again in case you didn't hear me. You. Are. Coming. With. Us."

"Who's us?" the other tall one said.

"I rarely go anywhere without my brother, everyone knows that. He's waiting in the hallway." George smiled. "Now get your arses out to our taxi before I drag you there by your cunting hair."

Chapter Nine

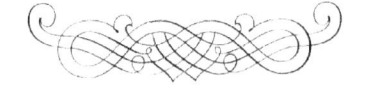

Roach had informed Betty that he'd had a word with Ezra, and the excruciating embarrassment of that revisited every time she saw her boss. Thankfully, it wasn't that often, because he left the running of the Orange Lantern mainly to her. Although saying that, his little lapdog, a woman called Precious, was probably there to keep an eye on her.

Precious interviewed any new women, deciding which ones got to work there. It was a little annoying because Widow felt it undermined her authority, but at the same time, she had to hand it to the girl, she could tell a good sex worker from a mile off.

Ezra must have been asking questions about where his mother could possibly work, and it seemed someone must have put two and two together and told him, because there he stood, opposite the Lantern, staring across with a deadly scowl and his hands in his hoody front pocket. She couldn't have him hanging around out there, nor should he be risking Roach seeing him, so she went outside and over the road to confront him.

"What the bloody hell are you doing *here?" she said.*

"I need some money."

What a fucking surprise. *She shook her head at him. Recently, he'd started to* look *like he took drugs. His face had that hollow appearance, and much as she didn't want to accuse him of going further with the gear than she'd ever imagined, she had a feeling her suspicions were right on the money.*

She studied him now, his defiant glare, his air of superiority. And was it wicked of her, but she wanted to slap his face. There he was, sponging off her, despite claiming to hate what she did for a living, but at least she was working. He acted as if he was the one with a decent job when all he did was loaf around for the most part.

"It's a shame that I don't even need to ask what the money's for," she snapped. "And I'm sick to death of handing it over, pretending to myself it's for the cleaning you do, when we both know it's to help feed your addiction. What sort of mother am I that I actually help you put drugs in your system? Shall I tell you why? Because when I see you all fucked up in pain when you go through withdrawal, I just want to make it go away. And because you won't go to that rehab place I told you about, what else am I supposed to do?"

"So can you lend me any or not?"

It was as if she hadn't spoken. She took a deep breath so she didn't bawl him out loudly and draw attention to herself from those in the reception room. "I don't happen to have it on me at the minute, and since you've been insisting on cash, then you'll have to wait until I do have it. And while you're here, I'm going to tell you this straight. If you ever come here again, in the busiest hours when Roach might turn up, you're seriously asking for trouble. I realise that when you're desperate for drugs you don't think straight, but he's not going to give a shit about that when he slits your throat for loitering about round here—oh, and annoying me, which he's explicitly told you not to do. I can't believe you have the bottle to ignore him."

"When can I have the money then? There must be loads in there with the punters handing it over to the slags."

"Don't call them that. And that money isn't mine, it's theirs. I can't just ask them to hand it over. What do you think my name is, Ezra Darlington?" She crossed over the road and said over her shoulder, "I mean it, you need to piss off and wait till I get home."

"But I'll get beaten up."

"Then maybe it'll teach you a lesson."

She went inside the Lantern, so angry that at the moment, if Roach came along and caught him, she thought it'd be no more than her son deserved. He'd changed even more in the past few weeks, the drugs taking a violent hold of him, gripping so hard he'd never be able to shake it off unless he went to that detox place. She was willing to fund it, too. She had plenty of savings now, not that Ezra knew about them. The last thing she wanted to do was advertise she had a fair few quid in a nest egg.

On top of Ezra being a pest—or more like an outright drain on her emotions—she still had Roach's murder to plot. If it wasn't for that man putting the drugs in the hands of the runner who sold it to Ezra, her son wouldn't be in this mess. Or maybe she ought to blame the college lads. If he'd never met them, again, none of this would be happening. If she hadn't insisted he went to college, all that. But then he'd been the one who'd suggested that, and university afterwards. At one time he'd wanted to better himself and have a good life. Unfortunately, meeting those boys meant her studious son had turned into one of those people she despised. One like his father had turned out to be.

But she could start with Roach to assuage her rage at how unfair this all was. But then wasn't that cutting off her nose to spite her face? If she killed Roach she wouldn't have this job and all the extra money. She'd have to go cap in hand to Indiana, but her old boss would welcome her back to the Bordello regardless. It would mean less wages and having sex again, but at least she wouldn't be touting her wares on the street corners or going on the dole. Who knew, maybe if she got lucky, on the night she killed Roach—from behind with a slice to the neck like he boasted he did to people, poetic justice—he'd have a wedge of drug money on him that she could take home with her, enough to pay for more than a month at the rehab place and get Ezra sorted out. It was time to make a stand.

How many times have I said that, though?

She got on with her work, supervising the goings on then having a chat with Precious while there was a lull in punters.

"So how are you finding the job?" Precious asked.

Aware she was probably asking so she could report back to Roach, Betty smiled. "I love it. The fact I don't have to go with any punters was a big draw. I did what I had to do to make money, but I can't say I enjoyed it, not like some of the women here. I do it for my son, you know."

"A lot of them do."

Curious, Betty asked, "Have you never thought of going down the route of renting a room upstairs?"

"God, no. That kind of job isn't for me. No disrespect."

"None taken. We all make decisions that are best for us. The job isn't suited to everybody."

Precious eyed her. "So how come you're still wearing your outfit from the Bordello?"

"I think it might be a safety net. I'm someone else when I wear the old-fashioned dresses, and when I take them off I become the me before I did all this kind of thing." She gestured to the kitchen, although that wasn't kitted out in flock wallpaper. It was the most modern room in the house.

"Did you do it because you have a child, or did he come after?"

Betty sensed she was fishing and she didn't appreciate it much. She wasn't about to bare her soul to this woman, only for her story to be repeated to Roach and Boycie and God knows who else. "It's something I prefer to keep private."

"Doesn't your husband or boyfriend mind?"

What the fuck is this woman on? Why won't she stop probing?

"I'm a single mother." Betty got up and moved towards the kettle. "Do you want a cuppa?"

"No, I'm going outside for some fresh air and to check… There was a kid hanging about across the street earlier. I'm wondering if he's getting the courage up to knock on the door so he can pop his cherry."

Precious' laughter churned Betty's stomach. That was her son she was referring to, as though it was a joke to discuss some lad's virginity like it meant nothing. To take her mind off wanting to go after her and punch her lights out, she got on with making her tea then took it to her office, checking her safe, even though no one else had the combination code, to make sure her nest egg was still there. It came to something when you preferred to leave your cash at work near a load of strangers than at home.

Her mobile rang, and she glanced at the screen. What did Lainey want? Betty swiped to answer, hoping her friend just needed a chat. "All right, love?"

"Um, I'm not working this evening, and I've not long watched your Ezra walk out of your house with that big telly you bought last week."

Betty's guts went south. That had set her back eight hundred quid, and she'd bet the little shit had stolen it so he could sell it and get the money he needed for drugs.

"Oh God," she said.

"Is he getting worse?" Lainey asked.

"There's no getting through to him. He was at the Lantern asking for money again, and I told him I didn't have it on me. He's obviously got the hump and gone home and nicked the telly."

"You could phone the police on him, Bets. I mean, that would really teach him a lesson, wouldn't it?"

"His own mum, grassing him up? That would make me look so bad. I'd be no better than my dad, turning my back on my child."

"Now don't get all lairy with me, because I'm not saying what your dad did is right, but sometimes, as a parent, we have to do things we don't want to. If I ring the Old Bill and say I saw him carrying that telly out, they'll take him down the nick and have a strong word

with him. It would shit him up enough that he'd stop what he was doing."

"Forgive me for being blunt, but you're naïve. He's not going to give two shifts, because all that's driving him is getting money for drugs. By the time he's picked up, he'll have probably injected it. He'll have got what he wanted and be in no fit state to understand the seriousness of what he's done."

"But he will when he's on the come down. There must be a part of him, the old him, who knows it's wrong. He needs a short, sharp shock, and this could be your chance to do it. The pigs might get the social involved, and that's to your advantage, because then he'll get the help he needs. Actually, you wouldn't even need to get involved. I'll ring it in now."

The thought of social services was awful, and would they even bother, seeing as Ezra was legally old enough to live by himself at sixteen? But if it got him off drugs, she'd suffer the shame. She nodded, then remembered Lainey wouldn't see it. "Okay, but it has to stay between us. I never want him to know that I was in on it."

"We've been friends for a long time, and there's no way I'd drop you in it with your kid. Like I said, this is for his own good. I'll speak to you later."

Betty slid her phone in her dress pocket. This was the first time anything big had gone missing from her home. The other stuff had been small, like her DAB radio and a bracelet that he'd have got fuck all for had he bothered to ask her how much it was worth. It cost her thirty quid from Elizabeth Duke a few years back. There must be other stuff he'd nicked, he probably picked things she wouldn't notice were missing, items she'd popped away in a drawer and forgotten about.

She didn't condone what he'd done, but at least with the little things it wasn't that much of a loss. But that telly had been her pride and joy. She'd been so chuffed she'd paid cash for it instead of getting one on the never-never. What hurt even more was that she'd told Ezra how proud she was, and it seemed he didn't give a royal fuck. He likely knew Roach was a good boss who paid well, and he'd see it as there was more where that came from and she could replace the TV, no sweat. She could, she could go and get one right now, but that wasn't the point.

He was sending her a message: If you don't give me the money when I ask for it, this is what you'll get.

She couldn't understand how drugs had changed him so much. He'd been an honest-to-goodness decent boy before. Kind and considerate. Mature, never talking back to her. He'd made her cups of tea when she'd got home from work at the Bordello if he was still up studying for his GCSEs. It was like he'd had a personality transplant, or his true soul had been sucked out of his body and the Devil had replaced it with his own. Night and fucking day, it was, and she was at a loss on what to do other than pray social services or the police stepped in.

Maybe the drugs brought out his true feelings. Up until he'd gone down that road, he might have hidden them, pretending to be the good son, when all along he'd felt how he did now. It seemed so long since they'd had a proper conversation, one that didn't involve money and her reprimanding him. How had it all gone so wrong? How had such a stable lad had his head turned? She never would have thought he'd have hung around with those types of boys, ever. It just wasn't him.

She locked her safe and went into the kitchen, leaving via the back door. She edged to the corner of the building so she could peer down the side and out the front. A couple of cars were out there, so new punters had arrived, but from her vantage point, she couldn't see Ezra, so she crept forward until she stood on the pavement. She glanced left and right, but he wasn't there. She knew he wouldn't be, but her stupid hope that Lainey had got it wrong had forced her out here.

"You absolute prat," she muttered and returned inside.

She'd get a phone call from the police soon, if they even bothered to pick him up. They might wait until tomorrow if they were busy elsewhere. A kid nicking a telly wasn't exactly high priority in London.

She caught a tear that dripped down her cheek. She'd been doing so well, all righteous that no one could say 'I told you so' about her having a child at a young age. Ezra had gone and proved everybody right by turning out to be the very boy they'd predicted he'd be.

Thanks for that, kid.

Chapter Ten

Ezra peered out the front from behind the living room curtain at the twins taking Rory and Ollie away. Those two hadn't even gone into the kitchen tonight—Kash had made sure he went to get any drinks and munchies as he didn't want them seeing the TV boxes, which were being collected at four a.m. According to Kash, the bloke they were being sold to hadn't been at the drop-off point when he'd arrived there earlier after abandoning Ezra outside the church. Marcus had decided to drive to Oxford instead, something had 'come up', but if he'd stuck to the plan, he'd be in possession of five flatscreens by now. Instead, The Brothers would be sending some men round to pick them up, so there'd be nothing for Marcus now.

"Rory and Ollie know fuck all," Ezra said, "and it won't be long before the twins realise that and come back for us. It's going to be obvious *us two* did the nicking."

"But we're not tall enough—even George said those two were the same height. I told you it'd work, didn't I. Stop panicking. I dumped the trainers, heel risers, and balaclavas, remember, before I took the van back. There's nothing linking us to those TV boxes because we didn't touch them without gloves on."

Ezra shook his head in consternation. "Like The Brothers do forensics and shit. They're not even going to *know* our prints aren't on the boxes, they're just going to assume they are."

Their taxi drove off, but Ezra remained at the window, watching out for whoever George and

Greg sent for the tellies. Were Rory and Ollie going to be tortured somewhere? The reality of exactly who the twins were had penetrated Ezra's brain at last. Why had it taken being confronted with those big bastards for him to accept they were frightening and people to avoid? Mum had warned him they were her bosses now, yet he'd still gone to the Lantern to get money off her, arrogant twat that he'd become, *and* he'd stolen TVs they'd donated.

What an absolute bellend.

"I *knew* I shouldn't have said yes to this," he mumbled. "I had a bad feeling something was going to go wrong, and it did. We've robbed the fucking church and won't even be getting paid for it because of Marcus fucking off, so whatever happens to us will have been for nothing. And what do we do if word gets out that the twins want to know who did it? They're bound to offer money as an incentive, and your mate with the van could come forward, not to mention the fuckers who want to buy the tellies off Marcus."

"Why don't you just calm down?"

Ezra turned to stare at him. "I know you've had a fair few hits on joints tonight, but come on, you can't *not* be scared."

Kash looked decidedly un-bothered. "We're safe. There's nothing anywhere to pin this on us apart from those boxes in the kitchen—which, if we're questioned, we'll say Rory and Ollie nicked, regardless of them denying it, which they will."

Ezra hated to admit it, but he'd throw those two under the bus if he had to, and, seeing as Kash was prepared to do the same thing, it brought home how he would blame it on Ezra, too, if push came to shove. Kash wasn't a friend, not the type Ezra had been led to believe, and Ezra wasn't one either. He was an arsehole.

He thought about going to the Lantern, confessing to Mum and being done with it, letting her tell the twins he'd been coerced into robbing or something, then he'd promise to move out of the house and get clean, go wherever the fuck she wanted him to so long as it was away from temptation.

Fuck it, yeah, that's what he'd do.

So he couldn't talk himself out of it, he went up to his room, stuffing some of his belongings into a backpack. He didn't have much, just clothes, a roll-on deodorant, and his toothbrush and paste. He put a few layers on because there was no more room in the bag, and, downstairs in the hallway, he popped his trainers and jacket on.

"Where the fuck are *you* off to?" Kash called.

"I need some fresh air."

"What am I supposed to do when the twins' blokes arrive to collect the tellies?"

"Do what you fucking like."

Ezra walked out and took the same route as he had on the way home from the robbery. He headed towards Our Lady. Maybe it was stupid of him to return to the scene of the crime, but it was on his way to the Lantern, and he was going to confess anyway and hope Mum could sway the twins' opinion of him so they'd go lenient on him, so what did it matter which way he went? Would he have bothered doing this if the robbery hadn't been reported to George and Greg yet? No. He'd likely have continued the way he was, working for Cooper, getting high, rinse and repeat. This could be divine intervention. He scoffed at the thought of God helping him out here, sending him towards his mother and a confession, saving his soul—or possibly damning it to Hell because the twins might not take pity on him. They could treat him as they would any other prick who'd dared to cross them.

Instead of taking the route that would lead him to the path directly outside Our Lady, Ezra crossed over so he could enter the park opposite. At least then he could see any activity from the safety of darkness—the twins were bound to have someone outside watching now, perhaps thinking the thieves would come back for all the other stuff in that storage room. He jammed his hands in his jacket pockets, pissed off Kash had taken his gloves and dumped them. His fingers were bloody cold, the tip of his nose freezing. He drew his hood up, cursing the fact he'd left his beanie behind.

"Bloody weather," he muttered.

"It *is* a bit cold, isn't it?"

The voice startled the shit out of Ezra, and he spun in a circle, trying to discern where it had come from. Then a shape loomed out of the dark, big goggles on the face, and he let out a shout of shock. Shit, it was the bloke from earlier, the one who'd stood by the van. Ezra reminded himself he'd had a balaclava on then, so he wouldn't be recognised now. Still, it was a bit unnerving to be in his presence again.

"What the fuck?"

"My name's Jason. What's yours?"

Ezra didn't want to answer.

"What are you doing here?" Jason asked.

"I'm walking to my mum's," Ezra said. "No crime against that, is there?"

"No. But a crime was committed earlier at the church. Someone stole all the tellies. I went home after, fell asleep for a little while and had a bad dream. When I woke up, I ran here because I'm going to catch them if they come back. There's a man over there in a car, he's watching the church, so maybe he's waiting for the chance to go back inside and steal something else. Don't know why he hasn't bought his van back, though."

Ezra glanced over at the road, making out the silhouette of someone sitting in the driver's seat of an average-sized vehicle. "Maybe the twins sent him."

"How do you know about them?"

Ezra shrugged. "The church is on their Estate, so it's obvious they'd be looking after it."

"Oh."

"Do you know who stole the TVs?" Ezra asked.

"They had balaclavas on. They were taller than you, and skinnier."

Glad he'd bulked up by layering his clothing, Ezra let out a long breath. "Did you ring the police?"

"No, but I went home and told my gran."

So maybe the gran had phoned The Brothers. If it hadn't been for this big weirdo here, the discovery of the theft wouldn't have happened until the priest entered the church in the morning. Ezra and Kash would have been home and dry once Marcus had turned up and taken the proof of the crime away. That was the trouble with life. People popped up in yours and changed the trajectory of where you were heading. They had some sway in how things turned out. Kash, Rory, and Ollie had done the same, and now this Jason. It was frustrating that Ezra had no control over what this man had done about tonight's bollocks.

"Anyway, I'd better get on," he said. "Mum will be wondering where I am."

"My gran does that, except she doesn't wonder where I am because she knows I'll be here. Our Lady is my favourite place in the whole world."

"Right. Yeah. So you come here most nights, do you?"

"And days, but I'm inside then. I help Father Donovan. I can't stay inside at night because he has to lock it up, so I've got my special goggles that help me see in the dark. I have to be home by eleven, though tonight I was late…" He reached up and tapped one of the lenses. "Everything looks black and green, and cats eyes are well creepy because they're like little balls of light. Come to think of it, the robbers' eyes were like that, too. It was weird because one of them ran away and I don't understand why. I wasn't going to hurt him or anything. Gran says I'm a bit big and scary, so maybe that was it."

"Maybe he got frightened because he didn't expect you to be standing by the van."

"I never told you I was standing by the van."

"Yes, you did."

"No, I didn't."

Ezra stalked off before the conversation escalated further. The bloke would probably twig something he shouldn't, and Ezra didn't want to be around when he did.

"Were you watching the robbery, too?" Jason called. "Only, I didn't see you in the dark. Have you got a special hiding place in the trees?"

Ezra ignored him and upped his pace, but not enough that he was running. For all he knew, Jason could be watching to see if his body movements matched those of earlier when he'd legged it. Look how paranoid he was now—Christ, if only he hadn't accepted the hands of friendship back in college, this wouldn't be happening.

Why did regret hurt so much?

Chapter Eleven

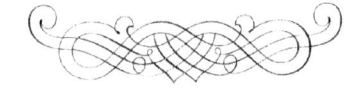

Gran would be cross if she woke up and found Jason gone. He'd crept out to the sound of her snoring. He'd be tired later, having his sleep broken, but in his nightmare, the church had been burned down, and he'd felt compelled to come out and keep an eye on it in case those people came back with matches.

He watched that man with the backpack until he disappeared into the tree line. *Was* he just coming through here on his way to see his mum, or had he come by to check if the police were outside the church? Wasn't it an odd time to be out visiting someone? Jason would remember what he looked like if he needed to describe him later, so for now, he put their meeting to the back of his mind.

He stared across at the man in the car. He ought to go over there really and ask him what he was doing, but what if he was a nasty person and had a gun or a knife? Jason didn't want to get hurt, but he didn't want anything to happen to Our Lady either. He made up his mind and stomped over the grass towards the path beside where the car was parked. He peered at the man inside, who stared back at him, giving him one of those looks Jason knew all too well, a: *What are you staring at, you freak?* He could say the same to this man—what was *he* doing here?—but the window was up and he wouldn't hear him speaking.

Jason made a gesture to either open the door or lower the window. The man frowned, and the glass sailed down.

"What the fuck's the problem?" the man asked. "And who the hell wanders round in the dark with goggles on?"

"My gran bought them for me," Jason said. "They were a birthday present in blue shiny paper. Why are you sitting outside the church in your car?"

"I'm looking after it for Father Donovan. The twins told me to come, so you'd best be telling me what you're doing here."

"I'm watching. I'm waiting for the robbers to come back. They stole some tellies earlier. I saw them."

"So you're the one, are you? In that case, the twins think you did a very good job, and they'll be wanting to thank you. Why don't you get yourself off home and get some sleep? I can keep watching till the morning and then someone else will take my place."

"I *am* a bit tired. Are you sure you'll look after Our Lady properly?"

"Yeah, I promise."

"And you're not going to go inside when I've gone and nick all the pop and crisps?"

"I don't know anything about any pop and crisps, mate. Honestly, hop it."

Jason sensed the man was telling the truth, so he nodded and headed towards home, going through the trees at the bottom of the park. Everything was so dark until the white of a face poked around the side of a tree trunk. It unnerved Jason for a moment, but then he remembered he was being James Bond so he was the bravest man on the planet.

"Oi, why are you hanging around here?" he called out.

The person seemed to fly out from behind the tree and head straight for him, arm raised and something in their hand. Whatever it was hit Jason's shoulder, and a harsh, ugly pain shot downwards inside him. The person stepped back, taking the thing out, and the pain grew more intense, hot, wet warmth spreading over Jason's skin. The green-and-white body in front of him with a black, stripy-tree-trunk background disorientated him for a moment, as well as the shock careening through his system. A sparkling flash of eyes, then a smudge of movement, a searing pain in the side of his neck. Jason went down to his knees, choking on liquid that tasted the same as when he licked the back of a metal spoon.

Blood.

The person ran towards the housing estate, and Jason struggled to turn his head; the knife was still lodged in his neck. He wanted to look back at the man in the car and flash his torch at him so he could see the light and come to help, but instead he pitched forward, gargling, heated blood spilling out of his mouth.

Gran was going to be ever so upset when he didn't make it home.

Chapter Twelve

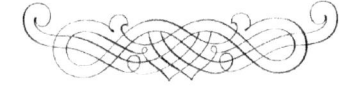

It hadn't taken long for George to realise that Rory and Ollie had no idea what the fuck he was talking about. Instead of taking them to the cottage, Greg had parked the taxi on the housing estate, and they'd walked them down the grassy bank underneath the river tunnel, then to the rear of their warehouse, climbing over the wall and entering through the back door. It was a fucking pest that CCTV had been installed out the front, and they'd made an agreement with Bennett, the CCTV man, that they wouldn't bother him to keep moving the cameras away from their particular warehouse unless they really had to. Since Launderette Lil had given them the cottage that their father, Ron Cardigan, had gifted to her many years ago, they'd barely been at the warehouse anyway.

Actually, George had an idea about that, so while Rory and Ollie sat roped to chairs after an intense scare session, he took his phone out and messaged Bennett.

GG: Double-checking there are no cameras at the backs of the warehouses.

Bennett: None there, no.

GG: Okay, warning you that something is going to happen in about five minutes, so if the front CCTV can be casually moved to point up the road rather than down it towards the housing estate…

Bennett: Just looked, it's already pointed that way. Not due to do an automatic sweep of the street for another twenty minutes. Is that long enough?

GG: It'll have to be.

He slipped his phone away and prowled the warehouse, going into the bathroom to collect several tracksuits they kept on the shelves for when they needed to change clothes, plus a few forensic suits. He dropped them in piles around the main warehouse, propping the bathroom door open with a small pyramid of towels. At the tool table, he bent beneath to take out the can used for the petrol that he put in one of his chainsaws. He'd had many a good time here, and some bad times, but he was about to put a permanent end to it.

Greg eyed up the can in George's hand. "Yeah, it's probably for the best. No point hanging on to something that's of no use to us anymore. Squatters will get in eventually, and we really don't need the police poking around."

"What's going on?" Rory asked, his gaze darting from the petrol can to the lighter between Greg's thumb and finger. "I swear we know nothing about the televisions. Please, I just want to go home."

"We believe you," George said. "but that still leaves us not knowing who took them. Your two other mates aren't tall enough, so who the hell else did you have at your house?"

There was, of course, the chance that their new surveillance man hadn't looked up in time to see where the men had exited from, which house, so he could have just assumed they'd come out of Ezra's—he might not have wanted to say he hadn't been fully concentrating on the job. This was the one time they could have done with Ichabod being out there, watching, but he'd made a fair and valid point recently that since Marleigh was pregnant, it was best that he take a step back and just run their casino. Ichabod had given some of the firm members pointers on how to go about stalking someone without detection, but to be honest, no one would ever be as good as their Irishman. Will was a close second, but he was currently off on holiday, taking a well-earned break.

"I don't remember anyone else being at our house," Ollie said. "But like we told you, we'd been to Rory's mum's for our dinner, then we came home and went to sleep. We wouldn't even know if Kash and Ezra went out. We woke up then went straight on the spliffs."

"Are you lot always fucked off your faces?" George shook his head. "Don't bother answering that. Now then, seeing as you already know how nasty I can be, I don't need to tell you that you need to keep your mouth shut about all this. You know nothing about the tellies going missing. You know nothing about this warehouse. You know nothing about anything, do you understand?"

"Okay, okay," Rory panted out. "Seriously, man, I just want to go home and forget everything."

"How about you forget the fact that you're friends with Ezra an' all? How about whoever's name is on the tenancy kicks him out. I don't want him being able to live with you anymore. Turn your back on him, make out you think he did the robbery, whatever it takes, you're not to have anything to do with him. If I catch you as much as looking at him, we'll come back for you, got it? Come on, I'm about to do something very upsetting, so get your arses out the back."

He helped Greg to untie them, then Greg handed the lighter over and took the lads out the back near the wall where they used to tip chopped-up body parts into the water. Christ, all the memories here… All the times he'd fucked people up, hurt them, killed them. All the regrets when he'd gone too far with those who didn't deserve the heavy treatment, and even more regrets for those he hadn't wounded enough. They really did need to find somewhere else to brutalise those who didn't play by the rules, because although the cottage had the steel room, there was only a certain amount of bodies that could fit in the pocket of space beneath. Not to mention the stench when they opened the trapdoor in the floor if a body had recently been dumped under there… He had to think of somewhere else the dead could be hidden.

He sprinkled some petrol on the towels, tracksuits, and forensic suits, then splashed some up the interior doors. He glanced over at where the steel rack on the wall used to be—they'd taken it down and planned to put it back up in the steel room. Many people had been manacled and abused on there, some left hanging overnight to think about their actions and the torture to come, then the death. His gaze landed on the original torture chair, wooden and scarred, such an integral part of what they did here. It would be the one thing that had shit loads of DNA on it, but he was still loath to let it burn. It'd be like letting go of their van, something that had been with them for years, part of the fabric of who they were.

It has to go. No room for sentimentality.

But wasn't it better that he disposed of it somewhere he could ensure it would burn down to ash? Much as he trusted Bennett not to alert the authorities about any smoke and flames he spotted until it was too late to save the place, he couldn't trust the other warehouse owners not to phone the fire brigade, and the flames might be seen from across the river and reported. The chair might not burn enough in time.

He was going to have to stand by the back door and wait until the last knockings before he closed it and left the area. He had to make sure the fire destroyed as much of the warehouse as possible, but then if the brigade arrived and hosed the place down, wouldn't the water destroy any evidence?

He sprinkled the remaining contents of the can over his circular saw and the rest of the tools they hadn't yet taken to the cottage. He put the lighter in the pocket of his forensic suit while he carried the chair out the back—he was so tempted to keep the bloody thing, but that was one risk too far. This was the end of an era, but everything changed eventually, and it had been on his mind far too much that the place had been left abandoned.

He picked up a pair of petrol-wet tracksuit bottoms and draped them over the edge of the tool table. He took the lighter out and flipped the wheel, the fabric catching quickly, a ball of flame erupting and snapping at his gloved fingers. He jumped back, moving to the door so he could open it enough that the oxygen would feed the flames. The orange and yellow tongues licked their way around the large space and crept towards him. He darted out the back, letting the door shut, then locked it.

He ignored Rory who whispered about getting away before the police came. "Or are you going to leave us here to take the blame?"

George stared up at the row of slim windows just below the eaves. That glass would blow out soon, and as the orange of the flames glowed through, he judged the fire had climbed up the walls enough that sufficient damage had been done to hide what had occurred here over the years.

He gripped the top rung of the back of the chair in one hand and Rory's arm in the other. "We'll drop you at the house. And remember, not a fucking word to Ezra and that other fella. Kash, isn't it?"

"Yeah," Rory said. "I'm actually thinking of seeing if my mum will have me back home."

"Good luck there," George said. "If you've been as much of a prick as Ezra has to his mum, then don't be surprised if you get short shrift. We'll be watching you lot from now on, and if I hear you've given your parents any gyp, you'd best be looking over your shoulder."

As they had reached the arch and voices would echo and carry beneath it, George shut up and manhandled Rory along the narrow path. He guided him up the embankment, remembering the time they'd helped that woman escape Ron Cardigan. She'd left London, taking the twins' sibling with her inside her extended belly. A ribbon of emotion fluttered through George. He didn't think he'd be upset, but as he glanced to his left at the warehouse and the windows shattering, he had an unexpected lump in his throat. He blinked the sting away from his eyes and gestured for the two scrotes to get in the back of the taxi. George put the wooden chair in the passenger seat then he got in the back with the druggies. Greg got in the driver's side, stared at the chair, shrugged, and put his seat belt on. He drove away, seeming unfazed by the destruction of the place where they'd spent a significant amount of their time.

George, on the other hand, struggled.

But at least there were still the memories, eh?

Chapter Thirteen

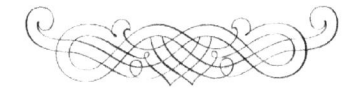

Ezra had sold Mum's telly to a skaghead in town who'd driven a hard bargain, but in the end, Ezra had scored enough money to get him two days' worth of heroin. He stuffed it in his coat pocket, ready to get home and use it. He rushed through the streets, desperate to get there, his head down and his hands in his pockets, the fingers of one curled around his stash.

He glanced up every so often to check his route, and once in his street he broke into a jog, lifting his head as he got to the garden gate. Something warned him of danger, except he wasn't sure how white could be dangerous, but it was the stripe down the side of the car that did it. Too late, he realised it was the police, one of them getting out of the driver's side and the other approaching from the front door, walking down the garden path towards him.

Shit, he had gear on him. What were they doing here? Had Mum finally had enough and grassed him up for being a druggie?

"Ezra Darlington?"

If they knew his name, then someone he knew must have phoned in about him.

"Yes…"

The officer who'd been at the front door asked him where he been, stating different times, and then Ezra knew what this was about. The television. One of the neighbours must have seen him with it. Lainey? He couldn't see her grassing on him, to be honest. She was kind and seemed to understand the hassle of being a teenager. Mum was at work, so it couldn't have been her. He'd bet it was that nosy bitch over the road—what was her name, Marjorie or some shit like that. Old bird. Hair in rollers.

"A witness saw you stealing a television from this property. Where is it now?"

"I never took no television." Ezra shrugged. *This was his first offence—the first one he'd got caught for anyway—so it wasn't like he'd be banged up in prison for months. He'd likely get a slap on the wrist and a talking-to from Mum, not that he'd listen to her.*

He thought about the money he'd got for it, how it was nothing near what the television was worth. Mum had been so proud of it, of being able to buy it with cash instead of on tick. As soon as he'd seen it delivered, he'd known he was going to steal it and her happiness would be short-lived. He'd turned into such an arsehole, plain and simple, and couldn't seem to stop himself from behaving this way.

He ended up in the back of a police car in cuffs, seeing as they'd searched him for sharp objects and found the heroin. He'd refused to say who he'd bought it from—there was no way he wanted to dob his supplier in—and he reckoned he'd get to sit in a cell as some form of punishment and then be let go in the morning, maybe sooner if it got busy later and they needed space for someone who'd actually committed a proper crime.

Being in the police station frightened him, all these questions when he was booked in, the copper behind the desk a bit brisk but the other two more pally-pally. They called him mate and had a joke with him. He didn't joke back in case it was a trick. For all he knew, they could be testing him to see if he gave any shits about what he'd done. He wanted to do as he was told and get the hell out of there. It went down on his sheet that he was in for theft and having a quantity of drugs 'on his person'.

After an hour in a holding cell, someone came to collect him. Being stuck in there all by himself meant it wasn't difficult to understand what it would be like if he had to do that for twenty-three hours a day if he was ever sent to the type of nick where you didn't get much free time. He supposed he'd be allowed books, but there was only so much reading you could do before that became boring. All he knew was that he didn't want to be stuck in here any longer than he had to be.

He followed a couple of plainclothes officers into a room, plus someone called an appropriate adult, seeing as they hadn't been able to get hold of Mum. He hadn't expected that, he thought the uniforms would have spoken to him, considering what he'd done wasn't exactly the crime of the century, but what did he know?

One of the coppers said something for the video recording and explained that the interview would be taped. He leaned back in his chair and folded his arms. Late thirties, thinning brown hair gelled back, beaky nose and beady eyes, the type that looked all pupil until you squinted and realised they were really dark brown. "The packaging on what you've told us is heroin is the same type as a strain we've been trying to trace the origin of."

Talk about diving right in... The statement stunned Ezra for a few seconds. Did he take it that they were more bothered about the drugs than the telly? And as for packaging...fucking hell, it was a two-by-two-inch zip seal bag, nothing fancy, unless you counted the white skull printed on it.

"Have you had that particular heroin before?" Thin Hair asked.

"No, it's usually in a plain baggie."

The other officer leaned forward. Strawberry nose, floppy black hair, and a belly that rivalled camel's humps, what with his trouser waistband being too tight and digging in. "You should thank your lucky stars you were arrested for nicking your mother's television this evening, because had you taken that heroin, you might not be alive by now."

Ezra frowned. "What are you on about?"

"There have been eleven hospitalisations and three deaths in the past two days," Thin Hair said. "Every

incident is linked to this heroin with the skull on the packet, so it's important you tell us where you got it from so we can trace then stop the supply."

"If you think you can walk up to them and say a couple of people have snuffed it and some have got poorly…" Ezra huffed out a laugh. "They're not going to care."

"That's your opinion. However, some dealers don't want to get done for murder and they'd appreciate being told their gear isn't top-notch. If we can at least give it a try, they may well stop handing out death sentences and let their *supplier know the drugs are killing people."*

"I can't tell you who it is because I don't know his name, and if I tell you where he sells from… Will he know it's me who's told on him? Like, would you tell him?"

"No, any information you give will be confidential."

Ezra spilled the beans. He reckoned the quicker he did that, the quicker they'd let him go. As for the close call with the heroin, he had the witness of the telly theft to thank for his lucky escape. Or was the thing about the heroin killing people a lie, a trick to get him to talk? It was too late now, he'd already given the name of the runner he'd bought from. The thing was, would Roach get information from the skagheads loyal to him, people who'd find out somehow that Ezra had been arrested? Would he put two and two together and realise Ezra had spoken to the pigs? All right, he hadn't given Roach's name, but he might as well have done. The runner may well open his mouth and give them that information.

"Do you know who supplies the drugs to that runner?" Thin Hair asked.

"Yeah, but I can't give you his name. He's already threatened me about keeping my gob shut. He's a right scary bastard, and if he finds out I snitched on him, he's got this mate who'll do me over. Even if he's in prison, that friend will take over the business."

"Can you at least tell me what he looks like?"

"No, because I don't actually know, I can swear to you on that one. They cover their mouths and they always wear sunglasses and put their hoods up. They use nicknames. I doubt anyone knows who they really are, but they're not the type you should cross. I could end up dead, know what I mean?"

"Why don't you get yourself out of this mess now, while you've still got a good chance of getting clean and starting your life again? You're young, and despite nicking a telly, you don't strike me as the type to do that on the regular."

"You sound like my mum."

"So maybe we've got a point. All I see is a young lad who's got caught up in something he probably thinks he can't get out of, when he can, because there's help available."

"Nah, you're all right."

Thin Hair sighed. "In light of what you've told us regarding the heroin, we'll give you a caution for the theft of the television. We'll give your mum a crime number so she can claim on the insurance."

"I don't know if she'll even have any."

"Well, don't you feel all kinds of bad, then?"

Ezra shrugged like he didn't care, but he did feel bad. "She earns enough, so she can buy a new one."

"What, so you can steal it?"

"I was desperate."

"And you'll no doubt be desperate again." Thin Hair shook his head. "Honestly, sort yourself out. It isn't fair on your mum having to keep paying out because you've got sticky fingers. Bear in mind that when word gets out that we're aware of the skull packets, the suppliers may well put the drugs in plain ones, so it'll be a lottery. You'll never know what you're going to get. The big supplier might not give a shit about people dying and they'll make out the drugs are a new batch when they're not. Unless each baggie

is tested, no one's going to know any different. Are you actually prepared to take that risk? We can't guarantee finding the source and destroying that particular batch."

Ezra had never thought about dodgy batches before, he'd always assumed the sellers would make sure the gear was good. All right, he expected it to be cut with certain things so it went further and they made more money out of it, but nothing harmful like the crap that was killing people. The trouble was, the heroin had such a hold on him that even though he knew it was super dangerous to take it now, his mind and body would force him to gamble with his life anyway—the pull was so strong that he could never ignore it.

"Seriously, kid, have a proper think about what you're doing to yourself. And think about how your mum feels. She's worked hard and bought a telly, only for you to flog it. She knows the money you got for it will end up in your veins, or however the hell you take your heroin. All she'll have ever wanted for you was a good life, and going by the state of your appearance, you're a couple of hits shy of turning into a proper lowlife. Get out now, while you've still got the look of guilt in your eyes, because believe me, when you go past that point, there's usually no turning back. If you want to hurt your mum for the rest of your life, then

keep doing what you're doing, but if she's a good sort, then she doesn't deserve what you're dishing out and you need to pack it in."

Black Hair had a look at something on Thin Hair's tablet. "I see you're still living at home with her — you're sixteen. How long before she kicks you out? Is she the type to do that?"

"No."

"Maybe not now, but when you turn into a supreme arsehole, which you will, she'll have to question whether she can continue having you under her roof. She may not want to let you go, but she might have to for her own sanity. We've seen it time and time again, lads like you being arrested, acting like they don't give a shit, and many of them don't, but you're different. You look like you can be saved. Would you like us to put you in contact with people who can help?"

Ezra had had enough of this conversation. Guilt piled up inside him, brick by heavy brick, and he felt stifled, eager to get out of this room. Out of the police station. He wasn't going to get his stash back. He'd stolen the telly for no reason, because he'd spent all the money on the confiscated baggies. In a couple of hours he'd be in a right state, desperate for a hit, but if he could get hold of Kash to see if he had enough gear to share, he'd be all right.

"Can I go home now, please?" he asked.

"Home. It might not be for long when your mum finds out what you've done."

Ezra was so sure she'd never kick him out that he brushed away Thin Hair's words. Mum would never see him out on the street no matter what he did, and, cruel as it was for him to play on her emotions like that, he'd continue to do it for as long as he had to. Heroin had turned him into a manipulative little bastard, and he couldn't seem to shake off this new personality. If Kash didn't have any spare gear, Ezra would root around the house to find something to steal.

He left the station two hours later after social services had been informed and Mum came in for a chat. Ezra had been cautioned; he'd have to pay a fine. That was a joke. Any spare cash she had went on drugs, so when the letter came, he'd leave it on the side and let Mum deal with it.

Outside on the pavement, Mum wiped her eyes. "What's **happened** *to you?"*

"Oh, fuck off, will you?"

"I'm going to have the social poking into my life now. Where I work, whether I'm a suitable parent. Do you realise what you've done, or don't you care?"

He glared at her. "I don't care." He did, but he wasn't going to tell her that.

He traipsed home—she'd probably return to her precious job. In Mum's bedroom he rifled around in her chest of drawers, then her built-in wardrobe, to see if there was any hidden jewellery. He'd done that before and had come up empty, and he came up empty again now.

Fuck it, he was going to have to get hold of Kash and grovel.

Chapter Fourteen

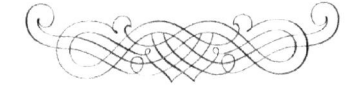

Betty hadn't expected the security guard to come up and get her, saying her son was outside. She'd recently told Ezra to text her if he wanted to see her, not to turn up at five a.m., and to never let anyone know who he was to her and why he waited outside. So why had he broken that golden rule? Maybe the twins had gone to speak to him and he'd come here to give her an apology, something George would likely have insisted on.

She stood opposite the Orange Lantern under a streetlamp, Ezra close enough for her to touch, but she didn't bother reaching out in case he shrugged her off. She felt awkward in her pyjamas and dressing gown with a coat over the top. Thankfully, her slippers were fur-lined booties, so only her head, face, and hands were cold. She could go and get warm, but there was no way she was asking him inside. She didn't trust him not to steal something from her apartment.

She'd purposely not brought any money out with her. She was done with helping him feed his habit. If the twins hadn't spoken to him already, he was going to get a short, sharp shock in the near future that Mummy wasn't a pushover anymore.

"Are you after money *again*?" she sniped.

"No, but I'll need some soon."

"What for?"

"I've left the house. I've had enough. I'm going to give up selling drugs and taking them and everything. I need your help."

Although stunned by what he'd said, Betty wished she could believe him, but he'd said this to her before and nothing had come of it. "I'll give you another hour and you'll be running back there." Uncharitable of her, but she was sick of pussyfooting around the truth in case she hurt his feelings when he didn't care about hurting hers. He said what he had to say, whether it was blunt and upsetting or not. It was about time he took a dose of his own medicine.

"I can't go back there, not now," he said.

"Why not?"

"Because the twins have been round."

She was going to make out she had no idea. George had suggested it was the best way for her to move forward. "What for? What have you done? They don't turn up at random." So she came off as totally authentic, she ranted, "If you've done something to fuck up my job… I've put up with it until now, but not anymore. You're an adult. You're old enough to understand what's right and wrong, so if there's consequences then you'll have to face them. It's got to be bad if they've rocked up at your gaff. I dread to think…" She still had a heart—seeing him shivering in the cold tugged at it. "*Tsk*. Wait there a minute while I go and get us a cup of tea."

"Can't I come inside?"

She thought about it. "Okay, but only my office downstairs. I won't have you in my private space, not with your light fingers."

He tutted but followed her across the road to the house. She dipped down the side and then around the back, going into the kitchen and holding the door open for him until he'd come in. She shut and locked it, going to the still-hot kettle, one that had a 'keep warm' function and showed what temperature it was at in a digital panel. It was at ninety-five, so that would do. She quickly made them a cuppa and caught him eyeing the biscuit tins on the sideboard. She'd adopted the same thing here as Indiana had at the Bordello—treats for the staff.

"Grab one of those and come with me." She carried the cups down the hallway and turned left into her office. She placed the tea on her desk, swivelling to find him already sitting in one of the chairs opposite.

"I need a wee." She locked him in the office but didn't go to the toilet. She messaged the twins.

Widow: What do I do? Ezra's turned up.

GG: Keep him talking. We'll come to collect.

She returned to the office, closed the door and locked it, thinking Ezra would have no qualms about emptying her safe if he knew it was inside one of those cupboards. Maybe he'd been nosing and already knew.

She sat and drew her tea towards her. "So what's been going on?"

He lifted his cup and wrapped his palms and fingers around it. How long had he been outside? Had he needed to get up the courage to knock on the front door? His hands must be frozen if he could stand his skin to be against the hot china.

"Kash said there was this job to do. Easy money. The twins had bought some televisions for this raffle. There's a fayre going on tomorrow at Our Lady, that church you used to go to as a kid. So anyway, I said I wasn't sure about it, but then I changed my mind because I was desperate for a fix and was running low on money. I had a bad feeling about it right up to the point we left the house, but Kash came up with this really good idea. He had these heel riser things that you put in your shoes to make you taller and bought some cheap trainers that were too big for us."

Betty didn't need him to explain the logic. She nodded. It *was* a good idea but not something she wished her son had been exposed to. It spoke of treachery and deceit, and she didn't like it. Nor how *she* was being deceitful by making out she didn't know what had gone on. It felt like her loyalty was now with the twins and not her own child.

"So anyway, he borrows this van off a mate, dunno who that is, and we go to the church and he's got a lock pick, so we get in quick. We take the tellies and put him in the van, and then there was this bloke. He was big and had these goggles on and he stared at us. I shit myself. Kash got in the van and fucked off. I thought he'd try to find me after I ran, but he didn't, he just went to drop the tellies off, but the bloke who was buying them wasn't there. I'd gone home at this point, shot up an' that. He'd put the tellies in the kitchen, saying the bloke would come round and get them later on. Then Rory and Ollie got up, and because they didn't know what we'd done, Kash was acting like a maid, keep getting the drinks and snacks so they didn't have to go in the kitchen."

The way he spoke reminded her of when he was little, going through every step and relating it to her, except back then it had been innocent stories about getting ice cream with a friend or going bowling.

He rubbed the end of his nose. "Next thing I know, the twins are there, and they got us all to stand up. Someone must have told them how tall the robbers were, because George picked out Rory and Ollie and took them off in a taxi. I said to Kash it won't be long before they know the other two didn't take the TVs. I left Kash at the house. Some blokes that work for the twins are going round to collect the tellies, and I wanted nothing to do with it so I came here. Then something else happened…oh, fucking hell…shit… I've got to stop this crap, Mum. You've got to lock me in a room or something so I can't get my hands on any drugs. If you don't help me, I'm going to end up in a worse mess."

Oh, so it would be *her* fault if she refused and he went down a darker path. He was making it a Mum problem, not his. Fucking charming. Thankful she could see her son for exactly who he was instead of kidding herself that he was a good lad, she asked, "Why did you tell me about this? Was it because you think I'll be able to persuade the twins to go easy on you? So you're basically using me?"

"Yeah, there's that, but for a while now I've been thinking I need to get away from that lot. I should never have made friends with them in the first place."

At least he'd been honest. While Betty felt sorry for him and she was relieved he'd apparently seen the light, she'd never trust him again and unfortunately saw things in black and white these days—less painful that way if you faced up to the truth. He was using her for his own gain, and she was well aware that if he wasn't in the shit, he wouldn't have come here. She was a means to an end. He didn't give a fuck about saying sorry for everything he'd put her through, just that she agreed to do what he wanted.

What a nasty little bastard.

How odd that this was what she'd prayed for, him desperate enough to turn to her again, but now she'd got it, she wasn't sure she wanted it. She'd stepped over the line where she'd forced her heart to harden, and it was going to take a lot for her to allow it to soften again.

"I'm not going to lock you up, there's rehab you can go to, and if you really want locking up, I'm sure George and Greg will accommodate you. As for me paving the way for you, the simple answer to that is no. I warned you that one day you'd push me too far, and unfortunately, that's the case now. Clearly, when you stole from me, you didn't get it into your head that that was the wrong thing to do. You stole other things and now televisions donated to a fucking raffle—and that's pretty unforgivable, nicking from the church."

"So you're going to kick me out of here and let me get on with it." He opened the biscuit tin and took out a bourbon. "I'm going to have no choice but to go back to the house. There's no one else who'd help me but you—and maybe the twins if you bothered to put in a good word."

Anger flared. Who the *fuck* did he think he was? "Would you listen to yourself? You've just tried to emotionally blackmail me—again—and I really am pig sick of it. You *chose* to leave home and go to live in that house. You *chose* to live the life you've been living. You're now selling drugs on the streets—that's a far cry from the career you planned when you were younger. How have you let three other people derail you so spectacularly? How come the opinions of these 'mates' means more to you than mine? How has a drug changed your personality to the point I don't like who you've become?"

He swallowed the biscuit he'd been chewing, his eyes going watery. Yes, what she'd said to him was harsh, but they were words she should have said a long time ago, and he needed to understand that although a mother's love should be unconditional, it wasn't always the case when the child was a selfish cunt. A mother had to safeguard her own emotions when they had a son who treated them so appallingly.

"Sorry," he said.

And she thought he meant it, too, until he tutted and rolled his eyes.

"You couldn't keep it up for long, could you?" she said. "Soon you'll be calling me a slag and all sorts because I won't do what you want. Maybe you've always had that trait and I chose not to see it. But the problem for you is, the veil has been ripped away, and I can see you for exactly who you are. I can't keep mourning the boy you used to be because he doesn't exist anymore, just like the mum I used to be doesn't exist anymore. We've both changed."

A tap on the door dragged her attention away from the top of Ezra's head where he'd dipped it, unable to look at her. "Who is it?" she called.

"Can I have a quick word?" the security guard asked.

She got up and unlocked the door, stepping out into the hallway and closing it behind her. The security guard jerked his head towards the front door where George and Greg stood. She walked over to them and whispered what Ezra had told her.

"Are you going to ask us to go easy on him?" George raised his eyebrows.

"I'm going to ask you to treat him how you think he needs to be treated." *May God forgive me, but he has to learn.*

"It sounds to me that he's remorseful for breaking into the church, so that's something. We'll have a quick word with him in your office. I'll soon see whether he's lying or not."

"If you're going to hurt him, I don't want it to be here," she said. "I don't want to know about it either. I couldn't cope with the guilt."

"Because of who he is and because of who you are, we're prepared to send him away to get help. However, if he comes back and fucks up again, there's no second chance."

Tears flooded her eyes, and she nodded. "Thank you. I'll…I'll just go up to bed now, but I doubt I'll get to sleep anytime soon."

"Leave him with us. We'll get to the bottom of it."

Chapter Fifteen

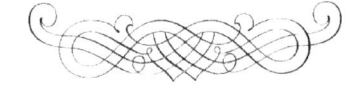

Ezra all but shit himself at the sight of the twins walking into Mum's office minus their blond and ginger hair and beards. He clutched the biscuit tin—as if *that* was going to save him—and then took a custard cream out and rammed it in his mouth to prevent his teeth from chattering. His stomach rolled over, and he couldn't stop his feet from tapping on the floor. Had Mum grassed him up? Had she messaged them when she was meant to be in the loo?

"You're going to drop those fucking biccies in a minute, and it'd be a shame for all those custard creams to land on the floor. I'm partial to those." George dipped his big hand into the tin and took five, strolling off to sit behind the desk.

Greg nabbed a couple of bourbons and sat in the spare chair.

"Your mum's gone off to bed," George said. "I've let her know what's been going on at Our Lady and whatnot, and you know what? She hasn't said a word about you being involved. Have you got any idea how precious it is to have a mother who'll cover your back? By rights, no matter who you are, she should be telling us what you've been up to—it's in the unwritten contract between us."

"Don't hurt her for keeping shit to herself."

"Don't tell me what I can and can't do." George munched on a custard cream. He seemed to take ages about it, too, as if he wanted the tension to grow. "I think you know who took those televisions but you're too scared to tell us. If I were in your shoes, I'd be too scared to tell us, too, considering we can be a right nasty pair of bastards, but the thing is, we happen to like your mum, she's a good sort, so we want to get this sorted out without any bloodshed."

Bloodshed? Fucking hell… But seriously? What had he expected?

Tell them the truth. "It was me. Me and Kash. Rory and Ollie didn't know anything about it, I swear. They didn't even know the tellies were in the kitchen because Kash wouldn't let them go in there. There's this bloke coming to pick them up, he's called Marcus, but then your fellas must have gone and picked them up by now, so that doesn't matter."

"Nah, we said that to make you think someone was coming. What's actually happened is a man's sitting outside the house, watching, and Greg is messaging him to let him know this Marcus is coming, so cheers for that information. What was your involvement?"

"Kash was the one who planned it all after he was asked if he could get his hands on any electrical goods. His sister goes to the church a lot. She's one of those do-gooders, and he was around his nan's house while she was there talking about you two buying televisions for the raffle. She said some bloke told her where they were being stored, and I reckon it's that Jason I saw on my way here."

George frowned. "Jason Ludlow?"

"I don't know what his surname is. He had goggles on and said he'd seen the robbery. He reckons he looks after the church in the evenings. There was this other bloke there, sitting in the car, and Jason thought it was one of the robbers who'd come back."

"No, he's one of ours. What time did you see Jason?"

"Literally minutes ago."

George looked at Greg. "He was supposedly in bed when the intel came in about what he'd seen."

Greg shrugged, lifting the last bourbon to hover it near his lips. "Maybe he went back out again if he's fanatical about keeping the place safe. James Bond, don't forget."

James Bond? What the fuck?

Ezra got twitchy, so he crammed another biscuit in his mouth. Greg used the phone again, probably sending a message, and George stared at the carpet, clearly thinking.

Ezra had another confession, but if he let it out, there was no going back. He'd keep it to himself for now—after all, the twins might let him go with a slap on the wrist, and seeing as Mum wasn't prepared to help him, he still needed somewhere to live. The fact that he'd seen Kash stabbing Jason in the trees… It'd really frightened him. He'd never seen something so violent before; he hadn't even thought Kash was capable of it. Yes, he was good at robbing and making a quick buck so he could score, but to actually *stab* someone? It had been horrific, and Ezra had felt really sorry for Jason who was one of those types Kash always took the piss out of. He hadn't deserve to die, especially in what had looked like a really painful way. The amount of blood had churned Ezra's stomach, and he'd had to force himself not to rush up to Jason and help. He'd also resisted ringing the police.

What had bothered Ezra was that Kash must have followed him from the house and he hadn't known it. He hadn't heard his footsteps or anything. While Ezra was talking to Jason, Kash must have crept into the trees. He'd eliminated the only witness, but what pissed Ezra off was that he hadn't hidden his face as he'd emerged from the tree line and walked through the estate to the Orange Lantern, so if anyone had seen him, they could give his description if a press conference went out when Jason was found. And he would be found. People walked through those trees all the time as a cut-through onto the estate, and then there were the dog walkers.

Would the twins think Ezra had done it when news filtered out about Jason's murder? Would he be interrogated to such a degree that to make the torture stop, he'd admit to killing him? It happened all the time, didn't it, false confessions?

"I've just sent him a message," Greg said

Those words pulled Ezra out of his head. He wasn't sure who'd been sent a message—the twins could have had a full-blown conversation just now and he wouldn't have known it.

"Who?" Ezra asked.

"Fuck me, cloth ears," George said, "our bloke outside the church."

A phone bleeped, and Greg read the screen. "He says Jason spoke to him earlier, and he sent him home."

"Good. That at least means we don't have to go out there and round him up and get him back to his gran." George shifted his attention to Ezra.

"So you took the tellies, Jason saw you, and then what?"

Ezra went through it all, right up until the present second, minus the murder. "I didn't want to do it, but I admit I wanted the money. These drugs are fucking with my head, man. I asked Mum for help, told her to lock me up, but she won't do it. I've pushed her too far, and she's had enough. I don't blame her either." Although he was hurt by it and wanted to hurt her back somehow, but he thought she was so over him that whatever he did or said wouldn't upset her. She probably expected him to hurt her some more so had prepared herself for it.

"It's not too late to turn things around," George said. "Make it right with her. And you've got your mother to thank for us being so lenient. We're prepared to send you away somewhere to get clean. It's up north. We have a friend called Jimmy. We'll get hold of him and ask him if he's got a job for you. I'll not beat around the bush: you're not welcome in London anymore. It's time to get out and start again, kid. If you're willing to do that, then we're willing to help—but only because your mother has become a good friend of ours."

George leaned back and rested an ankle on his knee. Ezra wanted to look away, worried he'd get accused of being rude by staring, but George carried on talking.

"Do you know she was prepared to kill Roach in order to get you off drugs? She took the job here so she'd be close enough to him to be able to murder him. Why she didn't, we don't know, but think about that, the level of her love. You're probably aware he snuffed it anyway, so someone else was pissed off enough with him to get there first, but she went from being prepared to kill someone to being prepared to walk away from you without looking back. *You* did that. You made her feelings go blank with regards to you, so I don't want to hear that you've sent her messages or emails from your new place, making her feel guilty for the choice she made this evening."

It felt like a weight had been lifted. Ezra doubted very much he'd got away with the theft, he'd have to pay somehow—maybe they felt the banishment was enough—and he was well aware it wasn't going to be easy coming off heroin. He had a long, tough road in his future, but at least he'd have a roof over his head and a job. He doubted the work would be legal, but maybe he could use it as a stopgap, something to get him through university, because he was going to apply to go. Despite fucking about in college, he'd got the required qualifications. He was going to rewind and start on the right path, see where it took him. Maybe if he made a success of himself, Mum would be able to stand seeing his face again.

"I'll do whatever you want," he said.

George smiled. "Well, there was a little something I wanted you to do for us, and it involves going back to the house as if nothing's happened."

Ezra didn't want to do that, because drugs would be available even if it was only sharing weed with one of the others, and now he'd made up his mind to break free, what if returning there set him back? What if he wanted to stay? What if he was persuaded to carry on doing what he'd been doing?

Don't be stupid, the twins aren't going to let *you stay, so you've got no choice but to do what they want then get the fuck out of London.*

"What do you need me to do?"

Greg held a finger up while reading his phone screen. "Hang on, there's no need for him to go back and let us know Kash is home. He's just turned up and he's talking to some bloke who's got a flatbed lorry." He glanced at Ezra. "Do you know who that is?"

"It could be Marcus or the man who works for him."

"Our man assumes he's coming to collect televisions. I've told him to follow the lorry if the tellies are taken away. We'll leave Kash thinking he's got away with it for now. In the meantime, we could do with getting some sleep." George looked at Ezra. "I don't trust you staying here to get a bit of kip, so we'll drop you off at a hotel we know. Someone will come by later with some methadone—that's as close to heroin as you're going to get now. If you go AWOL, we *will* find you, and the reception you'll get won't be as nice as the one you've just received. Put it this way, your mum might be picking out a coffin." He took a business card out of his pocket and tossed it on the desk so it skidded to the opposite edge.

Ezra put the biscuit tin down and picked the card up. It had a phone number on it and nothing else, so he put it into his contact list on his mobile while he was still lucid enough. The amount of adrenaline he had going through him had stopped him from crashing, but he could feel it coming. He needed to get to that hotel so he could sleep a few hours away.

"You wait for us to contact you," George said. "All your food and whatever will be paid for while you stay there. We need to arrange a room for you at a rehab place, but as you can imagine, we're fucking shattered, so it can wait. If Kash gets hold of you, let us know so we can round him up at some point tomorrow. We'll need you to text him. You can ask him where your cut is for the televisions and say you want to meet up to collect it."

"He'd tell me to go home and get it."

"Then you say you've gone to your mum's for a break and he'll have to meet you in a location of your choice. Then again, if he insists you go home, we'll drop you there in our taxi and you can say you're not stopping. We'll wait for you to come back out." George rubbed his forehead. "I'm too tired to work it all out now, but that's the gist of it. Come on, let's get you to the hotel. I don't know about you, but my dogs are barking."

Ezra had no idea what that meant, but he followed the twins out of the Orange Lantern and across the street to the BMW. He cringed. Most people knew that car was theirs, and if he was seen in the back of it by someone who knew Kash, they could tip him off that he'd been with the twins. He said as much to George as he got in the back.

"Lie down, then," George said.

Ezra did as he was told, his eyes drooping as the relief of having things taken out of his hands pushed him towards sleep. He'd been such a little dickhead for what felt like forever, and although he'd probably burned his bridges with Mum, hearing that she'd been prepared to hide what he'd done from The Brothers meant she still cared.

It meant there was still hope that she'd forgive him.

Chapter Sixteen

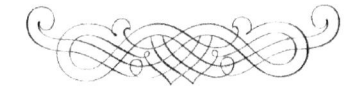

Betty had learned to live under the shadow of the social services. Like she'd explained to the nice woman, Ingrid, who came to visit once a week, her job was just a job. It didn't define her. It didn't mean she was a bad person. It put dinner on the table. And, of course, drugs in Ezra's system, although neither Betty nor Ingrid had openly acknowledged that by her giving

him money, Betty was actually feeding his habit and, by design, committing child abuse.

But it seemed today was the day to bring that out into the open as Ingrid said, "You're going to need to refuse to give him money. We both know he isn't going to buy a new pair of trainers like he says, or a coat, or to go to the cinema. Cruel as this sounds, if he wants money, he's going to have to get it for himself. A job, although he'll likely steal again instead. When I spoke to him last, he was belligerent and put up a brick wall."

"He only became a problem when he started hanging around with those lads."

"He said the same, so he does understand where it all went wrong. It's obvious to me that you've tried your best, and previous to him meeting those boys, Ezra was a decent kid. He's had his head turned, and unfortunately, it means I'm here to talk you through ways to help him."

"Which is, quite frankly, a waste of time because he won't listen to us. I've tried to talk him round. I've even offered to move away, for us to start again, but he threatens to move out. The thought of him living somewhere with that lot churns my stomach."

"But there's nothing you can do to stop him. Sadly, our children grow up and realise they have rights. While he's only young in our eyes, and incredibly

naïve about how the world works, he'll see himself as an adult. Do you think it would be of benefit if I offer him a place of his own? It would be a bedsit with a shared kitchen and bathroom and a house manager to oversee everything, but it's a clean house. What I mean by that is there's regular drug testing. You have to be clean in order to live there."

The thought of Ezra moving out hurt Betty's heart, but if it'd do him some good and get him back on the straight and narrow, she'd agree to anything. "He's old enough, or he thinks he is, to make up his own mind. You can put it to him, but I've got a feeling he won't agree. He doesn't seem to think he's addicted, or so he tells me anyway. All he's bothered about is getting money for his next hit. I used to moan about him smelling of marijuana, but I wish that was all he took now. It's gone too far, and I don't know how to bring him back."

"I'm coming to the end of my report," Ingrid said, "and from what I've seen, all of the decisions have been his own. I don't feel your job or your home has in any way impacted Ezra's decision-making, nor has his upbringing. I feel he wanted to be accepted in a group of lads and has done whatever it took to achieve that." She placed some leaflets on the coffee table. "Give those a read, see if they help."

Betty stared at them, the titles on the fronts something she never thought would relate to her.

How to Support My Addicted Child
When Drugs Rule Your family
Heroin the Homewrecker

Tears filled her eyes. "I honestly thought you'd have taken him away from me. It would have been for his own good if he'd been placed somewhere he had no access to drugs."

Ingrid nodded. "Sadly, because his home and you yourself are decent, it was advised by my seniors that he remain in place. Sending him to foster parents could have had an adverse effect."

"But I'm not talking about foster parents, I'm talking about rehab."

"There's no evidence he's taking heroin—as in, we have nothing tangible, just the police report that he had two baggies on him. He's told me he isn't addicted, and he refuses to show me his arms or other places where he could be injecting. You and I both know he's lying, his tweaking behaviour is a big indication, but I can't force him to admit anything. Plus with him being sixteen… Between me and you, you're actually lucky that we've had our sessions. Normally my boss would

have put Ezra down as a lost cause and told me not to bother—he's not young enough, not vulnerable enough compared to others who are being beaten and starved, that sort of thing. As much as it might not seem like it to you, your son's case is mild, and as he's old enough to live by himself, I wouldn't ordinarily have been sent out to try to help you."

Betty winced. The thought of children suffering like that was a bit too much for her at the moment. She wished Ezra could see how lucky he was to have her as his mother when so many had mums who didn't care about them. But no amount of talking to him seemed to get through—even Ingrid had struggled to get him to see sense. If Ezra had any guilty feelings regarding his behaviour, he had yet to show them. All Betty saw was that brick wall Ingrid had mentioned.

You could preach all you wanted, but your congregation didn't have to listen.

"So why did we even bother going through this?" Betty asked. "What made Ezra so special? Was he a box to tick? Proof that kids in normal suburban life are still prone to be drawn into the world of drugs?"

Ingrid had the grace to look sheepish. "Those police officers who spoke to him the night of the television theft really wanted to try and help him, so they pushed for an intervention. Like me, they believe that Ezra could go back to how he used to be if he was supported enough. Unfortunately, he has other ideas."

"I imagine because you're all stretched so thin that you can't afford to waste any more time on someone who isn't being receptive. It's so daft because like you say, me and my house are nothing to worry about. On paper, it looks like he's gone wayward and dabbled in drugs."

"That's exactly what it looks like, I'm afraid. Much as I'd love to stick around and coax Ezra into some form of rehabilitation, it's very doubtful it's going to happen. Legally, he could leave home now and there's nothing you can do about his actions. Another few months and he'll be seventeen and the social services won't want anything to do with him."

"So even if you did do all that hard work, by the time he was seventeen, you'd be pulled off the case anyway?"

"Most likely, yes. He then becomes a police problem if he continues to steal and whatnot. I didn't get the sense that he's the type of lad who'd hurt you in order to take your purse or your bank cards, but please be aware that even the most previously kind and gentle person can turn into a bit of a monster where drugs are concerned. There may come a point where you have to look out for yourself rather than look out for him."

Betty couldn't imagine doing that again, especially as the social intervention had basically done fuck all.

Ingrid went on. "Telling your friend to phone the police regarding the television theft was a good move because at least he now understands that his actions have consequences. However, I don't feel it scared him enough not to do it again. My worry is that you're now going to be in a vicious cycle and that one day you're going to need to make the decision as to whether he can live here or not. I don't envy you. I have children of my own, and it would be incredibly hard to turn any of mine away, but as I've seen how cases like Ezra's have escalated, there comes a time when the parents realise they cannot keep doing this. They accept that they bought their children up in a good and decent way and that the children have chosen to ignore those teachings."

Ingrid stood, and Betty got up to shake her hand. Although it had been embarrassing at first to have the social services coming to her doorstep, Betty had got over that by telling herself that only Lainey knew who this woman actually was. And then it got to the point where Betty looked forward to speaking to Ingrid, to a woman who understood that while Ezra presented as a little bastard, deep down, he was good.

"Of course," Ingrid said, taking her hand back so she could pick up her bag, "Ezra may move out of his own accord. That would be the best scenario for you, because there's no guilt on your part: you didn't tell him to leave, you didn't give up, you didn't admit defeat. I really hope things work out for you."

"Thank you, you've been very kind, and I'm sorry that it seems to have been a waste of your time. Ezra's not interested in going back to how he used to be."

Ingrid sighed. "Read that leaflet about the rehab place. Mention it to him as often as you can so it reinforces the fact that he does have help out there. He may not want it yet, but one day he could grab at it with both hands. There's another place called The Vines, but you'd have to pay for that yourself. It's around twenty thousand per month."

Betty said goodbye to Ingrid at the front door, a lump barging into her throat at the thought of coping with Ezra on her own again. It was only now that she realised how much of the burden Ingrid had taken from her shoulders just by listening to her once a week. She wanted to shout out to the woman and get her to come back, to ask her how to navigate this shitty part of her life, how to cope, how to tell herself that Ezra calling her a slag wasn't what he really thought of her, but he said it so often now that she could no longer convince herself that he was only saying it out of habit. He was being intentionally cruel and mean, no doubt about it, and if he wasn't her son, she'd have told him to get fucked ages ago. She'd have washed her hands of him, turned her back, and got on with a life by herself.

Part of her worried, though, that if she cut herself off from him, he'd go and find his grandparents. But her dad probably wouldn't even know who he was, and he'd likely shoo him away. She didn't want her boy to go through that, so she had a feeling she'd always keep her door open for him here.

But would she? She'd never thought she'd let Lainey phone the police on him but that had happened. She'd never thought she'd welcome social services into her home, desperate for their help, but that had also happened. Who knew in the future whether she might tell Ezra to get out of this house and never come back.

The replacement television was gone. Betty discovered it was missing when she'd walked into the living room to find an empty space on the cabinet. She sat on the floor and cried, her heart telling her to never buy a new TV again, not until Ezra was living elsewhere, but her head saying she had to ring the police on her own son.

Eyes swollen and throat sore, she stared at nothing, thinking about little Ezra and how sweet he used to be. Sometimes, when she looked at him, she could still see that small boy in the roundness of his cheeks or the pout of his bottom lip. How quickly children changed, growing into unrecognisable people, unlikable people. She'd always love him but didn't like who he'd become.

It had been six months since Ingrid's last visit. Ezra was now seventeen, so phoning the police and reporting the theft and her suspicions that he'd stolen from her could have a very different outcome to the last episode — there might be more than a fine this time.

She pushed herself up off the floor and scooped her bag up, taking it into the kitchen and putting it on the table. She opened it and removed her phone, sending him a text message rather than phoning him as he would be unlikely pick up for her anyway.

MUM: DID YOU TAKE THE TELLY AGAIN?

EZRA: YEAH.

MUM: ARE YOU PREPARED TO FACE THE CONSEQUENCES?

EZRA: FUCK OFF.

Although he was probably high and that could be used as an excuse for what he'd typed, his responses still stung, and anyway, she reckoned being on drugs was the same as when you were drunk. People tended to tell the truth then; all his inhibitions were at least loosened in that he felt he could say what was in his heart, even though he might acknowledge on some level that it was wrong.

She huffed out a wry laugh at the fact that this television had lasted a lot longer than she'd thought it would. She'd risked buying it as a test, to see if he was that far gone he'd pinch it as soon as it had been taken out of the box. Before that, even. Because time had gone by, that told her he'd at least still had some part of him that knew stealing it so soon would be really wrong.

"It's really wrong no matter when *he nicked it," she muttered and sent Lainey a text to see if she was free for a chat. Her mobile rang a few seconds after she'd pressed* SEND, *Lainey's name on the screen.*

"What's he done now?" her friend asked.

"He's taken the other telly."

"What are you going to do about it?"

"I should phone the police really, especially because he's admitted it to me on a text. He's not bothered. It's like he doesn't care about anything except getting hold of drugs."

"I'd grass him up. It's the only way he's going to learn."

Betty wanted to scream at Lainey's usual response but held it back, saying calmly, "Like I said, he doesn't care, so why would *he learn? He knows I'll pay any fines."*

"Then you need to let him know you won't. He can get in the shit for not handing over the money. He's old enough now to face the consequences of his actions. If you keep making it easy for him, he'll keep doing it."

"That's okay for you to say because you're not the one involved in all this. I just…" While Betty could see Lainey was right, it was fucking difficult to do what needed to be done when you knew guilt would pay you a visit and weigh so heavy.

But was guilt a good enough reason for her to continue indulging someone who didn't give a fiddler's fuck how *he got what he wanted, only that he did? It was selfish of Betty to always obey her boy just because it was easier on her conscience. There had to come a time when she said, "No more!" and let the chips fall where they may—for his sake as well as hers.*

Chapter Seventeen

With the tellies loaded on the flatbed lorry beneath tarpaulin and Kash paid off, Moody drove towards his boss' lock-up. It was unusual for Marcus not to be around to oversee delivery of something worth so much, and Moody didn't know why he'd hightailed it to Oxford, but as he was being paid extra for working unsociable hours, he wasn't exactly complaining. Yeah, he'd had to get out of bed and leave his wife at home snuggled under the duvet, none the wiser that he'd even slipped out of the house, and there was the fact that the heating in the lorry was up the swanny so he was a bit nippy, but he'd soon get warmed up once he was home again.

Headlights in the rearview mirror piqued his interest, especially as it was ten past four in the morning. They'd been there ever since he'd left the pickup point, and while that didn't necessarily mean anything suspicious (someone could be on their way to work), he'd still be careful. If they were there when it came to the turning for the lock-up, then he'd sail past and drive to a secluded spot to see if they had the balls to approach him.

Unless Kash had told someone to follow him and steal the TVs back, Moody didn't think he had anything much to worry about, not when it came to using the gun tucked in the holster on his waistband. Weapons always spoke louder than words, and he'd sooner shoot someone in the forehead than stand there gassing—conversations were overrated.

As it happened, the car behind nipped down a side street, a Beemer coming out of the same one and taking its place. Moody's stomach did a funny little spasm—*The Brothers drive a BMW*—but he doubted very much those two would be out at this time of the morning, not when they'd got themselves so well established on the Estate and they'd have minions to do middle-of-the-night jobs for them. Anyway, the driver and passenger silhouettes looked nothing like the twins, and Moody should know, because he'd seen them around often enough.

He wished he could work with them, but whenever they'd had a recruitment drive, he'd always heard about it too late. He supposed he could have gone directly to them and asked for a try-out, but he didn't quite have enough bollocks to be so bold, so he'd ended up being Marcus' lackey. It wasn't so bad, he got paid well enough, and apart from not getting much of a chance to beat the shit out of people like he would if he was with the twins, he reckoned he ought to be grateful he had a relatively quiet working life, all things considered.

He continued on and turned into the road that led to the lock-up. He checked the rearview mirror, and the BMW continued on the road he'd just been on. He parked around the back of the lock-up building which was close to reception and the roller-door, garage-type effort Marcus rented. He put the pin code into the pad, and the mechanism released, the door itself scooting upwards too slowly for his liking, but as he'd found on a previous attempt to hurry it up by pushing it, the bloody thing jammed.

Instead of standing there doing nothing, he went to the back of the lorry and undid the ties securing the tarpaulin. He peeled the material back to expose the television boxes, then flipped down the tailgate and pulled one box towards him. The door had finished rising, so he got on with taking each television inside. At the point he'd put the last one down, he picked up on the faint sound of crunching, which to his trained ear indicated the soles of shoes scuffing loose debris on the tarmac. He turned to find himself face to face with two large men whose silhouetted head shapes resembled those in the BMW.

They stepped into the light coming out of the lock-up, and he got a good look at them. One with a long beard and matching ginger hair. One with long blond hair and a short, mousy beard. Both had black, thick-framed glasses and were the size of brick shithouses. One held a tyre iron, the other a knife. They could likely harm him with those weapons before he'd even had a chance to get his gun out, but he could still wound them with a bullet eventually, depending how hard he was hit with that tyre iron. If they had anything about them, they'd go for his head.

His courage flickered for a moment, its flame threatening to go out, and he thought of the wife at home and how she'd feel if she was told he'd been murdered.

"'Ere, I don't want any trouble," Moody said. "There's cameras, just so you're aware." He wasn't bothered about being caught on film shooting these two—the lock-up place was managed by Marcus' brother, and any dodgy footage was always disposed of.

"We couldn't give a single fuck about cameras," the ginger one said. "And if you're thinking of using that gun hiding under that jumper of yours, then think again. My name's George Wilkes, and this is my brother, Greg. Those televisions belong to us. Some cunt stole them out of the church where they were being stored, and as you can imagine, we're not best pleased about it."

Moody held both hands up. "Hang on. I didn't know they belonged to you. All I was asked to do was collect them from some kid. I don't know the ins and outs of what went on."

"Who told you to collect them and bring them here?" Greg asked.

"My boss."

"And who might that be?"

Moody sighed. "His name's Marcus Rupert. He works out of a Portakabin down Spruce Road, got a gaff at twenty-eight Parson's View. He buys and sells goods, that's all I know. I'm just his fella who goes round collecting whatever he's bought and bringing it here, then I deliver it to whoever buys it. I wasn't aware he dealt in dodgy goods, I thought they were legit transactions."

"And now that you *are* aware, what are you going to do?"

"He can stick his job up his fucking arse, can't he. If he told me what he was up to in the first place, then I'd have had the choice as to whether I still worked for him, but he's lied all this time, and that's pissed me off."

"Where is he at the moment?" George asked. "And please don't fuck us about by making out you don't know when you do, because we were supposed to go to bed ages ago, and then we got the call that you'd turned up at Kash's house and had clocked the car following you, so as you can understand, us having to come out and take over…we're knackered and not in the best of moods."

"He had to go to Oxford, but he'll be back soon. So he said anyway. I do as I'm told." Moody glanced across at the televisions. "I mean, if they're yours, I'm not going to argue with you if you take them away."

"We won't be doing that. We'll wait for him to sell them on, catch him in the act, so to speak. Do you know if he already has buyers?"

"Yeah, some blokes down your new pub."

"The Grey Suits?"

"Yeah, they bought them as surprises for their wives' Christmas boxes."

George glanced at Greg. "So not only did he get someone to nick off us, he organised the buyers in our fucking boozer. The cheeky… We'd be bastards if the women didn't get their presents…"

Greg nodded. "The sale can go ahead. We'll deal with Marcus afterwards. As for you…" He stared at Moody. "Marcus is going to find himself in a bit of bother soon, and it'll mean you'll be out of a job. He hasn't been paying us protection money, and he'll soon learn the consequences of that. We'll swap phone numbers with you, and you're going to tell us when he comes here. Once that's done and we catch him, you'll be in need of a new job, won't you?"

Moody had never listened to his wife's belief that fate played a big part in your life, but to be fair, she might well have a point. He'd wanted to work for The Brothers for years, and now look, they were offering him a job—weren't they?

"That's very kind of you," he said, "but Marcus will get me to collect the televisions and drop them off to the buyers. He never does shit for himself."

"Who else works for him?"

"No one, only me, unless you count the bully boys he always goes on about when I don't ask him how high I should jump. He doesn't like it if I can't fit a job in—you know, because I have an actual life."

"So if you're poorly, like you happen to get the shits, then he'd have to come here to collect the televisions, wouldn't he?"

"Marcus hasn't employed anyone else before, but it doesn't mean he won't start if I'm out of action. It's a busy time, what with Christmas around the corner, and I've got a lot of work on with collections and deliveries. If you're wanting to catch him picking up the goods, it might not happen. He's got a lot of mates who could step into my shoes."

Greg sighed and stared at his brother. "Can we not just stop this fucking about and go and get Marcus after the televisions have been delivered? We know he's the one who wanted them nicked. We know he's involved. We don't have to actually catch him at it. I want to go to fucking bed."

George nodded. "Yeah, we were making things a bit complicated there." He smiled at Moody. "I think you'll enjoy working for us, don't you?"

Moody nodded. "I'll tell him tomorrow I've got another job."

"We'll get hold of you to arrange a time to meet and discuss what you'll be doing for us. You spotted the car behind you, didn't you? And then you spotted us…"

"Yeah…"

"It's those types of observational skills we happen to need. Our number one surveillance man has had to step back, and while he's given pointers to a few men who're taking his place, it doesn't hurt to have more on the books. What's your name and address?"

"Alex Moody, sixteen Medina Gardens. I prefer to be called Moody, though, never did like my first name."

George took an envelope out of the inside pocket of his suit jacket. "Right, Moody, that should tide you over in wages until we've had our chat."

It felt thick enough to be a couple of grand in tenners, so Moody was happy with that. "I really ought to be doing something for this money, though. It doesn't seem right to take it and not be working."

"You're doing enough by not working for Marcus."

They turned and melted into the darkness, leaving Moody to flip the light off inside the lock-up and set the roller door in motion. He'd have thought they'd have wanted to take the televisions back if they weren't going to bother catching Marcus in the act, but maybe it was more important to them that five female residents got the Christmas present of their dreams. He'd heard the twins were nice under the hard exterior, and when he got into the lorry and switched the internal light on to check the contents of the envelope, he understood just how nice they were.

Twenty-pound notes, five grand.

Christmas was going to be a good one this year.

Chapter Eighteen

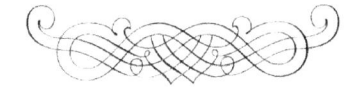

The unexpected phone call regarding the flatbed lorry driver being too vigilant had come just as George and Greg had begun to drop off into the Land of Nod. Moody had cottoned on to being followed, so Greg had suggested they take over, and they'd hastily slung some clothes and disguises on and intercepted the two-vehicle convoy, George effing and blinding about still having no kip, Greg telling him to shut his face.

Now, Greg drove towards home, and George sent messages to their relevant surveillance men in a group chat—as they'd be doing shifts, there were a fair few members.

GG: Keep any eye on Rory and Ollie to make sure they move out of that house. Leave Kash alone—we'll deal with him at some point. Keep observing outside the hotel to make sure Ezra doesn't leave to score drugs—if he does, he's forfeited our help and will be treated the same as Kash.

He then switched to their three-man hacking team.

GG: Don't care which one of you does it, but I need a check on an Alex/Alexander Moody, sixteen Medina Gardens, ASAP. He looks to be in his forties. Also, Marcus Rupert, twenty-eight Parson's View. Dig deep. Cheers.

He repeated the request in the chat called Coppers.

At last, they'd reached home again, parked in their garage, and stumbled into the kitchen, bleary-eyed. George set the alarm, and they once again went upstairs. George undressed and got into bed, his eyes gritty, and unfortunately, his brain wide awake again.

"I've got to say this shit out loud," he called out so Greg could hear him.

"Fucking hell, I knew I should have shut my door…"

George smiled in the darkness, avoiding looking at the clock; he didn't want to see how hideous the time was. "Right, if Rory and Ollie pack up and go home, they're in the clear. I don't think they're going to fuck us about, so we can basically scrub them off our list. Ezra: if he stays at the hotel and takes the methadone, we can arrange for him to go and work for Jimmy. If he throws our help back in our faces, he can suffer interrogation at the cottage, a fucking good kicking, plus kneecapping. I'm not pissing about here, this going behind our back crap has to be stopped. Kash…we round him up whenever. Moody—hopefully he'll turn out to be clean and someone we can use. As for Marcus…who the hell does he think he is? How many people has he robbed to then sell it on?"

"I could really do with talking about this tomorrow, bruv…"

"Yeah, but—"

"My eyes are closing…"

George kept his mouth shut and let his mind wander. Once again, he was hacked off that people didn't find him and Greg as frightening as they should. Why weren't they scarier than Ron Cardigan? Or were they, but people these days had more bollocks to ignore the rules? There was always going to be an element who kicked back and refused to conform. Fucking hell, if he wasn't a leader, he'd have been one of the first people refusing to play ball. He got it, he understood, but these rules weren't new. They'd been around for decades. George supposed they'd have to keep picking off the rule-dodging perpetrators one by one every time they appeared on the radar.

At least it'd keep them busy and it allowed his Mad side some freedom when they finally caught up with the cheeky bastards.

He closed his eyes, the sensation of his body sinking into the mattress taking over him. He allowed sleep to claim him, dragging him under into a world where he met a faceless Marcus Rupert and killed him by smacking him on the head with a flatscreen TV over and over again.

Surveillance 1: Rory and Ollie have left the house with suitcases and backpacks in a taxi. Rory dropped off first, then Ollie. Both at parents' homes.

That pleased George. It saved him having to catch up with them and give them another reminder—along with a few punches to the face.

GG: Cheers. Go and get some kip and take today and tomorrow off.

He read down the screen a bit further.

Surveillance 3: Ezra still in hotel. Has ordered room service breakfast.

GG: Your relief is on the way, should be with you in ten.

Surveillance 2: Kash still in house.

George gave that the thumbs-up and sent a text to Ezra.

GG: Oi, how are you doing?

Ezra: Bit shaky but okay. Kash has got hold of me, asking when I'm going home to collect my cut of the money. I've said I'm staying with Mum. He said Rory and Ollie have moved out and we'll need to find two more people else we can't afford to pay the rent.

GG: The rent isn't your problem anymore, and it won't be his for much longer.

Ezra: Shit, are you going to kill him?

GG: Nope, but he'll likely be in the care of the NHS for a bit. The same will apply to you if you fuck us over.

Ezra: By doing what?

GG: Leaving the hotel to score. More methadone will arrive in a bit — been informed you were only given 2mg when we dropped you off to tide you over. Our doc says you can now have 10mg, and the amounts will get higher and higher as the treatment progresses at the rehab place. Do you think you can handle it?

Ezra: I've got no choice. It's behave or you two do me over.

GG: At least you're under no illusion. Enjoy your room service breakfast.

Ezra: How did you know? Actually, don't tell me, it's obvious I'm being watched. Is my mum okay?

GG: No idea, haven't exactly had time to speak to her again yet. Why don't you message her and find out? You should hear from us by this afternoon. I've sent a message to the rehab woman, waiting on a reply. Hold tight.

George had better get something straight before he forgot. He got hold of Cooper.

GG: Ezra will no longer be working for you. Keep this to yourself, but he's leaving London.

Cooper: Okay.

Next, George messaged Jimmy a more detailed synopsis of what was going on. Yesterday, it had been a quick: Do you have a job for when a druggie gets clean? To which Jimmy had replied: Yes. It felt better to explain it all properly, leaving out names, of course, but George had no reason to doubt Jimmy or mistrust him, but still, best to use the pay-as-you-go burner and keep identities safe.

Jimmy: How long will he be at rehab?

GG: No idea yet. It's usually thirty days, but I think sixty will serve this kid better. I want him to do a course in relapse prevention while he's there. So let's say he'll need a job by the end of February. Something that can be done alongside university.

Jimmy: I'll have a chat with him in the next day or two, see what he wants to do with his life.

George sent Ezra's number over then let the lad know Jimmy would be contacting him.

Ezra: What about?

GG: Uni, that sort of shit. What job you'd be better suited to. Where you'll live. The future can be bright if you let it shine.

Ezra: Thanks. For everything.

GG: Don't thank me until you've kicked the habit. Got to go. Things to do. Talk soon.

One last message.

Moody: I've handed in my notice.

GG: Good man.

With the messages all dealt with and a clearer head now he'd had some sleep, George went into the kitchen, following the scent of bacon and the sound of the whirring fan in the Ninja. He glanced at the clock—ten a.m.—and sat at the island.

Greg made him a coffee from their Tassimo and passed the cup over, then got on with cracking eggs into a bowl for an omelette they'd likely share. "Any news?"

George explained what was what. "So now we can eat our breakfast in peace then nip to Currys for the new tellies. We'll get one of our blokes to take them to the church and stay with them in a van. I don't want to risk some bastard nicking them again."

"I doubt anyone would when they know we could turn up any minute."

"True. I'm looking forward to getting hold of Kash after the fayre and asking him how he found out the tellies were in the church. It'll be interesting to see if he tells us the truth about getting the info from his sister."

Greg poured ten eggs into a large frying pan. "I'm sure being strung up naked in the steel room will loosen his tongue. Plus he's young and inexperienced, so it won't take much to break him down. What kind of hospital treatment will he be getting? A basic operation on broken kneecaps or will he need rehabilitation to walk again?"

"I haven't made my mind up yet, I'll see how arsey I am when I've got the hammer in my hand. He'll soon see that being addicted to drugs means you make stupid decisions and you have to pay the price eventually."

"I wonder if he's already bought a load of drugs with his half of the money."

"I suppose we could always ask Cooper whether his runner has seen Kash recently, but to be honest, I can't really be bothered. We'll get the money off him, or what's left of it, when we go to pick him up."

"And how are we doing that? Just breezing into the house?"

"Yeah, we'll go in the same way we did last time." George shrugged. "Wigs and beards, our little van, we'll be golden."

The Ninja bleeped at the same time Greg turned the omelette over. Toast popped, and George got plates and cutlery out. They ate their breakfast, George staring out of the window over the sink, gauging the weather. It was one of those deceptive scenes where the sun was out, the sky was bright blue, but he'd bet it was cold enough to freeze the balls off a brass monkey.

Breakfast over, Greg loaded the dishwasher and George collected new beards and wigs. Their work phone bleeped in his pocket, and he took it out. Notifications in two WhatsApp groups.

SURVEILLANCE 4: MARCUS RUPERT AT LOCK-UP WITH FLATBED LORRY. NO SIGN OF A HELPER. HE DOESN'T LOOK HAPPY.

GG: PROBABLY BECAUSE HIS EMPLOYEE TOLD HIM TO STUFF HIS JOB UP HIS ARSE. KEEP WATCHING. THOSE TELLIES SHOULD GO TO SOME BLOKES WHO DRINK AT THE GREY SUITS, ALTHOUGH I HAVE NO

IDEA WHETHER THE DELIVERIES WILL BE MADE AT THEIR HOMES OR THE PUB. REPORT BACK ONCE THE TVS HAVE BEEN GIVEN TO THE BUYERS.

He moved to the group conversation that contained Colin and Anaisha.

ANAISHA: ALEXANDER MOODY HAS NO CONVICTIONS, NOT EVEN A PARKING TICKET.

GG: THANKS.

So George's instinct had been right to offer the man a job.

ANAISHA: MARCUS RUPERT WAS DONE FOR LOW-LEVEL THEFT WHEN YOUNGER BUT NOTHING FOR FIFTEEN YEARS.

So he'd learned how to not get caught, that was all.

GG: THANKS AGAIN.

Wigs, beards, and overalls on, a new decal on the side of the van, plus a fake plate. George took to the wheel this time. Greg browsed their work phone, which saved George the bother of having to repeat what he'd found out.

"So where are we off to first?" Greg asked.

"I'm in the mood to pop in on Kash." George smiled and put his foot down. He couldn't wait to get his hands on that little twat and hurt some truth out of him.

Chapter Nineteen

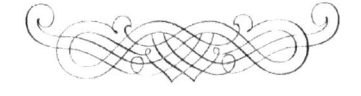

Kash was surprised Ezra didn't need his half of the payment as soon as possible, but maybe if he was staying with Mummy, she was shelling out for all of his gear. That woman blew hot and cold, so God knew why Ezra had bothered going to visit her. Kash could have sworn they'd fallen out recently, but maybe they'd made up again. He could just about keep a track on his own life, let alone anyone else's.

He worked out how many days were left before the rent was due. Two more weeks. With Rory and Ollie gone, only paying for the days they'd been at the house this month, there was a shortfall. Kash took his phone out and messaged Marcus to see if there were any more jobs on offer.

The lack of a quick response bothered him. Marcus was usually on the ball with shit like that. Maybe he was still stuck in Oxford doing God knew what.

He texted Ezra again, letting him know he'd be keeping the TV money for the rent—unless they could get two more people to move into the house pretty sharpish. He phoned around a few friends from college, decent types who had jobs, but only one was interested in renting a room. It would have to do. Splitting the rent three ways was better than two. The kid would be around later to have a look and see if he wanted to live there.

Kash's phone bleeped.

EZRA: CHANGE OF PLAN. I'M GOING TO REHAB. KEEP THE TV MONEY AS MY PART OF THE RENT. I'M NOT COMING BACK.

Kash could have screamed.

KASH: BUT WHAT ABOUT ALL YOUR STUFF?

EZRA: I TOOK EVERYTHING I NEEDED. THERE'S NOT MUCH ELSE LEFT IN MY ROOM. DUMP IT.

KASH: THAT MEANS I'VE GOT TO FIND TWO MORE PEOPLE TO LIVE HERE. I'VE ALREADY GOT ONE KID COMING ROUND, BUT NO ONE ELSE WANTS TO KNOW. THANKS A LOT, DICKHEAD.

EZRA: GOT TO GET MYSELF OFF THE DRUGS FOR GOOD. I'LL BE GOING TO UNI IN SEPTEMBER.

KASH: THAT'S AGES AWAY. WHAT ARE YOU GOING TO DO IN BETWEEN, LIVE OFF YOUR SLAG MOTHER?

EZRA: FUCK YOU.

Kash hadn't expected that response. Ezra was always the first to put his mother down, so he must have had an extreme change of heart to have reacted that way. Kash shrugged and got back on the phone, getting hold of the same people but asking them if *they* knew of anyone who'd need a room.

A knock at the front door pulled him away from a text string to go and answer it. Halfway down the hallway, he stopped and watched the front door open. Had Rory or Ollie come back?

Had they knocked out of politeness, then remembered they still had a key?

A man entered, followed by another who closed the door behind them. It was those fucking men from last night, The Brothers, and Kash closed his eyes momentarily, trying to keep his fear from escalating. Why were they in overalls? His mind wandered to when Rory and Ollie had gathered their things earlier. Neither of them had said a word to Kash about an upcoming visit from these two, like they'd been warned off speaking to him ever again. They'd taken their stuff and then got into a taxi, and a text had said they'd paid some rent into the landlord's account and wouldn't be coming back.

Had the twins told them to do that?

"Morning," George said. "We've come to take you for a little ride in our van. You can leave your phone behind, you won't be needing it."

Kash's stomach rolled over. "Where to?"

"You'll see when we take the blindfold off once we get there."

"Blindfold?"

This was sounding more ominous by the minute, and Kash worked out his choices. Go with them and blame the theft on Ezra in the hope they'd let him come home like they had with Rory and Ollie. Or run out the back way and get a bus up north to go and stay with his nan. Since he'd left college, he'd done nothing but piss about working at Home Bargains and smoking spliffs every evening.

But would he get away from these two in time? Yes, if he could manage to get out of the back door in the kitchen and lock it after him. The houses were terraces with no alleys in between, so they'd have to get in their van and drive round to the next street and hope they could catch up with him, but in an ideal world he'd be long gone.

"Yeah, a blindfold," George said. "We don't like people knowing where we hold our interrogations."

The moment for running had come and gone, and what George had said sounded promising anyway. If they were going to kill him, they wouldn't care whether he saw the location or not, would they, so maybe they were only going to ask him about the church robbery.

But why would they think Kash had anything to do with it when he'd used the heel risers to make himself taller? He was much too short to have been one of the thieves, and now he'd come to think of it, he couldn't blame Ezra because without the risers, *he* wasn't tall enough either.

"We're going to cuff you," George said. "Wrists behind your back so you can't take the blindfold off, although I suppose if you were clever you could rub your head on the side of the van until the material lifted. I really wouldn't advise that, though, because I'll get my brother to stop the van, and I'll climb in the back and stick your eyelids down with duct tape, and when I rip them off again, you'll probably be minus eyelashes, which I imagine would be pretty sore."

Trembling, Kash turned around so his back faced the twins. He was going to go through whatever they wanted; he'd come out on the other side eventually. He touched his wrist together at the small of his back, waiting for cold metal handcuffs against his skin, but something cool and skinny pressed there, and when it drew tight, the sound of multiple dulled clicks told him they'd used a cable tie. Next, a blindfold came from behind and covered his eyes, and he was at the mercy of two nutters.

"Won't the neighbours think it's weird that you're taking me outside like this?"

"We don't really give much of a fuck *what* your neighbours think," George said. "But you don't have to worry yourself about them. Our man who's been sitting in his car by the kerb will be paying them a visit to let them know that your little walk of shame down the garden path wasn't seen by any of them, if you catch my drift."

Kash caught it all right. They were going to be told to keep their mouths shut or else. Maybe that meant he couldn't talk about it when he got back either, not that he chatted with any of his neighbours, but this time they might take it upon themselves to come over and ask him if he was okay. Then again, he doubted it. If you were taken off by The Brothers, then they'd automatically think he'd done something wrong and he'd be given a wide berth.

They led him outside, and he hated having to rely on them to know where to put his feet when going down the two steps to the front garden. The sound of the gate opening reminded him he was supposed to ring the landlord about having it fixed. The hinges had dropped, and the left-hand edge scraped on the path. This wasn't something he should be worrying about. He should be more bothered about his destination, but maybe it was better to distract himself with the ordinary things in life rather than dwell on what might happen later.

Like his nan used to say, worrying about something never changed the outcome, so all the anxiety produced from swirling thoughts was a waste of time and only served to make you feel like shit.

He stumbled down what he assumed was the kerb, his knee bashing into something—the edge of the van floor? One of them lifted him inside, telling him to dip his head, then they guided him to a seat he suspected was a wheel arch. Doors slammed. Footsteps. Doors opening, slamming again, then the engine rumbling to life. Kash wanted to say something but wasn't sure what would be appropriate. He couldn't afford to set the twins off. They hadn't seemed particularly angry, but they could be hiding their true feelings until they got to the location.

"It's just a few questions and some persuasion," George said, "in case you were wondering."

Kash jumped; he hadn't been expecting the voice, plus the word *persuasion* didn't sound very nice in this context. Still, it wasn't like he could stop them from persuading him to do anything, was it? He'd willingly let them cuff him, and now he regretted not running. He could have been on the bus to Nan's by now if he'd got a move on and acted on his first impulse. On his way through the dining area, he could have thrown a few of the chairs and knocked the table over to stop them from being able to follow. But it was all very well thinking about what he could have done in hindsight when he was stuck in the back of a fucking van on his way to fuck knows where.

Chapter Twenty

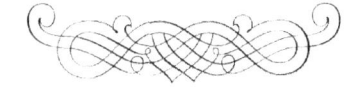

George paced in front of a naked and strung-up Kash, a nip to the air in the steel room. "Just a warning. Because of your little scam with our tellies, we haven't had much sleep. We were out and about in the early hours, following some bloke to a lock-up, so based on the few hours we *did* get, I'm feeling like a bit of a grumpy bastard."

He actually felt okay, but he wanted to unnerve the fucker. "So with that said, when I ask you a question, I advise you to answer me truthfully. No fucking about, no lying, and everything will be fine. Well, not fine, exactly, but you won't end up dead if my arsey persona comes out and takes over—unless my brother can't pull me off you in time. But anyway…"

Kash nodded, his face pale.

"Good lad. What can you tell me about Marcus Rupert?"

"I do jobs for him sometimes."

"Like nicking our televisions."

"Yeah."

"And you thought that was all right, did you? Well, clearly you did, otherwise you wouldn't have done it, or are you going to tell me you were forced into it; you broke into that church thinking that if you didn't, you'd be hurt, or worse, killed."

"No, it wasn't like that. It's how I earn my money other than being on the till in Home Bargains. I nick a few things, and he sells them on. My mate lends me his van—he's got no idea what I use it for, I swear. Marcus gets hold of me when he needs help."

"Explain the height issue to me. You're not tall enough to be who our man saw leaving your gaff."

"I've got these things to put inside the shoes, makes you taller. I bought some cheap trainers two sizes too big in case we left footprints."

"We."

"Yeah, me and Ezra."

"D'you know, I've got to hand it to you. I thought you were going to bullshit me and make out it was Ezra with a friend of his, but the fact you've admitted you were involved… I've kind of got a bit more respect for you. Not a lot, but enough that it means I won't completely smash up your kneecaps. I'll give them a good wallop, but not with the hammer. A rubber mallet will do enough that you'll find it difficult to walk without any pain for a while. How does that sound? Generous? Fair?"

Kash looked like he didn't agree with any of it but said, "Yeah, that's fair."

There wasn't much else the kid *could* say really, was there; the punishment was going to happen anyway. There was a resignment to his expression; he knew he was fucked. He was going to hurt more than he'd ever hurt before, and he was likely wondering how he was going to get home if they didn't take him.

"We'll help you get your clothes back on," George said, "we're nice like that. And we'll give you a lift to a spot near a hospital, but other than that, you're on your own. Do you get on well with your mum and dad?"

"Not really."

"Why, because you've been a little prick to them?"

"Yeah."

"Well, you'd better hope they've got some forgiveness in them, because you're going to need some help in the coming weeks. See, there's ligaments and cartilage in knees, and they're really going to get fucked up. You're not going to be able to get up and down the stairs easily. You'll need help going for a piss and shit. With your housemates all fucking off and leaving you in the lurch, unless you can find three new ones, you've got no choice but to give notice to your landlord that you're moving out of that house and going crawling to your parents. It's a small price to pay compared to what I could do to you."

George went over to the tool table and selected the heavy mallet, slapping it against his palm.

Kash seemed mesmerised by it, blinking every time the rubber met George's glove with a harsh noise. George got a kick out of freaking him out, but he kept his smirk to himself, preferring to appear serious. He doubted very much Kash would do anything against them again. He didn't seem the type to have the bollocks for a second bite of the pie, but stranger things had happened, so George reckoned he'd give him another warning to be on the safe side.

"Just so you know, if you work for Marcus again, it'll be more than your kneecaps that get hurt. I might decide to chop off your hands and every other bit of your body that sticks out, you know, ears, nose, lips, cock. You get the gist. And if you ignore me again after *that*, I'll saw you into one-inch pieces while you're still alive. You'll pass out from the pain, but I'll keep going and then pop your body parts in plastic tubs, load them into the van, and dump them in the river. Or I could kill you in your bed, no bells and whistles about it."

"I swear I won't work for anyone like that again. I'll never do anything bad."

Kash closed his eyes. George wasn't in the mood to insist the lad watched what he was doing. He thought he'd be in a worse mood than he was, but he found himself wanting to get this lesson over and done with. They had the church fayre to go to, and he wanted a fried breakfast first. He'd suggest to Greg they paid a visit to their new pub to see whether the managers, married couple Kenny and Liz Feldon, had noticed any dodgy shenanigans going on. Mind you, if they had, they'd have reported it—that's what they were paid to do. They felt they owed George and Greg because the twins had found who'd killed their teenage son in the hairdresser shooting.

George swung the mallet back then whipped it forward through the air. It connected with the right knee, a sickening crunch following, Kash's scream tacked onto the end. The kid kept screaming, eyes scrunched so tight, fists clenched hard. The veins on the undersides of his wrists stood out, as did the ones on his neck. He gritted his teeth, lips pulled back, gums going white. Without giving him time to recover in any way, shape, or form, George drew the mallet back again and gave the other knee a good wallop. This time something cracked, and the skin over the kneecap split, a spear of bone sticking out.

George turned to Greg and shouted, "Shit, I didn't mean to do that."

"Rehabilitation it is then," Greg shouted back.

Kash continued to wail in agony. George crouched to inspect the mess of the second knee. Blood spurted then dribbled down the shin. The other one grew swollen and red, the skin stretching so tightly it looked like it might tear by itself. George stood, a bit annoyed with himself because he'd been too heavy-handed, but what was done was done, and he couldn't change it now.

While Kash reconciled himself with what had happened, George jerked his head at Greg to let him know they ought to have a coffee break. If he didn't get some caffeine inside him he was likely to become more sluggish. They sat at the table in the kitchen with their drinks, dunking biscuits and eating them in companionable silence. It was nice to sit there without having to talk, to soak up the perfection of the moment, where nothing called to George inside his head and he could just be for a few minutes.

Interlude over, they returned to the steel room, and George explained what would happen next. They'd drop him off in a secluded area and get one of their crew to use a throwaway burner to phone 999 with the location. The SIM card would be disposed of, leaving no trace of who'd made the call. George was aware that his signature kneecapping could point to this being him, something he'd done as a teenager and then a young man, along with Cheshire grins, but Kash knew what was good for him. He knew not to blab.

"I'll say I was mugged," Kash gasped out. "I didn't see anyone's face, they attacked me and nicked my phone."

George wanted to brain him, end his sorry little life just for being so thick. "Think about what you said. How can they nick your phone *when you left it at home*?" he roared in his face. "Fuck me, you were at the back of the queue when they were handing out IQs."

"Shit…"

A flare of anger surged inside George. "You need to watch yourself, son. It seems to me there's a high risk of you saying the wrong thing, and if you do and we hear about it, we'll find you and rough you up even more—for fun before I chop you up into bits. Tell me your story again."

"I went out for a walk, and two blokes jumped me. They hurt my knees, then nicked some money out of my pocket. They put me in a car and took me somewhere, telling me someone would phone for an ambulance."

If he could have put his hands together in prayer, he would have, George reckoned.

Kash stared at George as if pleading. "That's it. That's all I know. I swear to God, I don't know anything else."

"All right, there's no need to act it out now. I'm not the fucking police, you dickhead. Now, I'm going to be kind to you and carry you back to the van. It would be fun to watch you dragging yourself outside, but we don't want you taking any evidence with you, so the less you touch the better."

Greg used the winch to lower the chains, and George stood ready for Kash to drape over one of his shoulders. The kid cried out as his knees rested against George's lower stomach, then came the tinkle of the manacles; Greg undid them. George held Kash while Greg managed to get him dressed and pop a blindfold on, tying his wrists behind his back. George popped him in the back of the van, imagining how much pain he was in and whether it would hopefully teach him a fucking big lesson. Greg secured the cottage, and he drove off, George in the passenger seat messaging Bennett and John to see which one of them was on shift tonight manning the CCTV.

Bennett responded and agreed to switch off cameras along one of the main roads they would have to take to get to the secluded location. Other than that, there was no CCTV in the vicinity. Greg parked up, and George got out to heft Kash towards a clump of trees where he propped him against a trunk, snipped off the cable tie, and stuffed it in his pocket along with the blindfold. It was pretty fucking nippy out, but Kash would just have to put up with it, especially as George and Greg needed to get away from the closest mobile mast for when they sent a message to the crew on another throwaway burner. Thirty minutes down the road, and George gave the go-ahead for the 999 call to be made.

"Do you think he'll remember to stick to the story?" Greg asked.

"He could fuck up, but so long as our names aren't mentioned, I'm not really fussed what he says. There was never any proof that I kneecapped people back in the day, only the usual bullshit rumours, but it still makes me uneasy whenever we leave somebody near a hospital for them to be picked up."

"Then why kneecap him if you're worried about it?"

"Dunno."

"Christ, you make no sense sometimes."

"I just like doing it, all right? It brings back memories of when we worked for Ron and we didn't have to do anything but be bullies. Now, we're governed by the Estate and all the fucking rules, and every now and then I like to indulge." George rested his head back, folded his arms, and closed his eyes.

"You'd better not be rude and fall asleep," Greg said.

"I'm just resting my eyes."

"A likely sodding story."

George smiled.

Chapter Twenty-One

Ezra had at least learned his lesson: he wasn't going to steal from Mum anymore. She hadn't paid the fine, sticking to her guns and saying he'd have to pay it out of his benefits, and seeing as it was only a fiver a week, he'd got on with it. Saying that, "only" five pounds a week was a lot when you were a desperate junkie, and at times, he'd struggled to get enough money together for a hit.

He'd got a job helping out on a building site, conning Tom, the bloke who managed it, to feel sorry for him. He'd made out he was homeless, sleeping in a bus shelter round the corner, and that he needed cash for food. Tom had said if he could sweep and tidy up, maybe pass a few tools to the workers when they asked him to, he'd give him fifty quid for an afternoon's work. At first, Ezra had gone there every afternoon for a week—Pavlov's dog theory at its finest: work coupled with the response of wages, which in turn meant heroin, ensured he'd behaved himself. But then he'd overslept, or he'd gone off somewhere with Kash, fucking about in the pub and getting rat-arsed when they only had enough money for booze. The buzz from a couple of pints was better than no buzz at all.

For ages after he'd grassed the drug runner up to the police, he'd worried that Roach would find out it was him, but although there had been whispers on the streets about Roach and Boycie being on the lookout for a snitch, no one had approached Ezra about it. The skull baggies seemed to have disappeared—had the suppliers actually listened to the police about potentially being had up on murder charges? Ezra had chanced it and bought some more heroin from his regular runner, who, as rumour had it, had been arrested for supplying drugs but for some reason was set free afterwards. Ezra had assumed the runner had given some information in return for being released, but there was no way he could strike up a conversation about it without putting himself in the shit. He didn't want to risk slipping up and saying he'd done the same thing.

He was feeling pretty good today. He'd been living with the lads from college for a while now, and he'd never admit he missed his mum, or her cooking, or the clean washing. He missed her voice an' all, the way she whinged at him to get off the gear and go to rehab. When he was short of a bob or two, he turned up at where she worked, praying she'd see him through a window and come outside. Sometimes she didn't, and he told himself it was because she'd been too busy to notice him. He didn't want to entertain the fact that she may well have clocked him but had decided to leave him there on his own.

When she did come out, they rowed about the money he asked for, and he could understand it because Kash had been sniffing around his arse for money lately, especially when he knew Ezra had been at the building site. The constant requests for dosh got on his nerves, yet he was doing the same thing to his mother.

Everything was so fucked up. He was the pot calling the kettle black, he was the pain in the arse, he was the mess people crossed the road to avoid. He'd seen Lainey the other week, and even she'd veered the other way, when usually she stopped to talk and ask him if he was okay. It was like those coppers had predicted: he'd become someone nobody wanted to interact with, a known druggie, a pest, a burden, his face gaunt, his body skinny, his clothes hanging off him. There was a time, if he'd have remained clean, when he'd have stared at himself as he was now, and shaken his head at the state of him.

He trudged on towards the building site, timing it for when the men brought out their lunch boxes. A couple of them offered to share food with him, but Tom normally nipped to the chippy down the road and bought him pie and chips. Ezra rarely fed himself. If he did, it was packets of Doritos or Mr Kipling's cakes, something easy to take out of the packet and ram in his mouth. He wasn't hungry a lot of the time, but when he was, he was ravenous, as if his stomach had hollowed out and hadn't had any food in it for months.

He turned onto the building site and smiled at all the men. They either sat in their cars with the doors open or on the garden wall of one of the houses being built. Most of them had their T-shirts off. It was a hot summer, and the peaks of baseball caps shielded their faces from the relentless sun. Tom wasn't there, so he must have already gone to the chippy—fuck, Ezra hadn't timed it right today.

The man with viper tattoos up both arms, Snaky his name was, passed him one of his sandwiches and half of a large pork pie. Ezra sat on the dirty ground and accepted the food, sitting there as though he belonged, when really he was only tolerated or pitied. It was sometimes difficult to look at himself objectively and see what he'd become, some stinky vagabond type with no prospects and an addiction that meant he'd never have any even if he wanted them, but today it was easy, his lens so clear.

"You might want to make yourself scarce if you've been up to no good lately," Snaky said.

Ezra squinted at him. "How come?"

"Got ourselves a body, haven't we. The digger's not long revealed it. The ground was packed tight, so it's been under the ground a fair while, but it's bones. Could be a dog, of course, but I'm willing to bet it isn't. I know a human femur when I see one."

Gavin, sitting beside Snaky, smirked. "Well, then you're either a weirdo or you've actually seen a femur before."

Snaky sniffed. "Dug up a body on another job. Ten years ago, almost to the day, as it happens. It was some girl. She'd been missing after a night out. The poor cow had her throat slit."

"Was that a body or bones?" Gavin asked.

"It was an actual body."

"So that makes no sense as to why you'd know a femur when you saw one."

Snaky tutted. "Shut up and let me tell you what happened. It was a shallow grave. The thing was, it was common knowledge that we were going to be building on that field, so that says to me the killer wanted her found."

"Unless they weren't local and they didn't know anything about it becoming a building site." Gavin took a swig of his Coke from a two-litre bottle. "Fucking hell, this sort of shit really gives me the creeps." He glanced over his shoulder, perhaps in the direction of where the bones had been found. "My mum did warn me that this type of bollocks could happen in my job, but I didn't listen."

Snaky nodded. "Mums say a lot of things, and at the time we think we know it all, but when we look back, we actually realise we knew jack shit."

If Ezra didn't know better, he'd say Snaky had been told to say those words, but they were just one of life's weird coincidences. "I wish I'd listened to my mum."

"Why didn't you?" Gavin asked.

"Because… I don't know, she got on my nerves. Loads of reasons. I wanted to do my own thing, to be myself in my own right, and it went a bit wrong."

"Did you end up in a bad crowd?" Snaky asked. "Because forgive me for sounding an arsehole, but half the time we see you, you look like a bag of shit. Whatever you're on, you need to stop taking it."

The same old words from those who'd never been addicted. He'd heard them too many times to count. No one could understand the pull of drugs if they'd never experienced it. It wasn't as simple as snapping out of it or deciding to quit.

Gavin snorted. "Hey, if this is the second body discovered where you've worked, you might be a prime suspect."

Snaky shook his head. "You really are a dickhead sometimes."

"What? It's true! They'll look into you, I'm telling you."

Ezra glanced away to look at the entrance of the building site. Tom entered carrying a brown paper bag of chip packets, a police car slowly nudging into the area where the tradesmen's cars and vans were parked.

"Here we go, plod's turned up," Snaky muttered from the side of his mouth.

Gavin jerked his head at Ezra but kept his gaze on Snaky. "He's going to have to stay and be questioned, isn't he. If he walks off now it's going to look weird."

Ezra shrugged and ate the sandwich. What did he care if he was questioned? He knew nothing about bones, so there was fuck all for him to worry about.

Tom approached and handed out the packets to those who'd bought chips. He glanced at Ezra and nodded. Seeing he had food, he sat and got on with eating his own. Ezra chewed on the pork pie next, listening to the coppers asking questions and the workers answering them. When it came to his turn, everyone agreed that Ezra had not long rolled up for work.

They'd had his back, stood up for him, which was more than Rory, Ollie, and Kash did these days. They treated him like an afterthought, like they regretted bringing him into the fold.

Maybe he should go cold turkey, get himself off the gear and work for Tom every day. All day, not just the odd afternoon. Labouring was a far cry from the career he'd wanted for himself when he was younger, but there was no shame in it, it was honest hard graft and a damn sight better than him poncing off the government for benefits. Or off his mother.

It was at times like this, when he felt like he belonged, if only for a few minutes, that he could see what needed to be done and what he needed to change in order to live a normal life, but as soon as the nudge came from the drugs leaving his system, that agonised call for a top-up, his perception changed. He'd soon forget all about who those bones belonged to, and the poor bitch whose body had been found a decade ago. They wouldn't feature in his thoughts at all, forgotten as the need for heroin took over.

He glanced around at the workers, a tight-knit bunch who would support him, he reckoned, if he asked for their help. What if he went to The Vine like Mum had said? What if he allowed himself to stay there for thirty days in order to get clean?

Did he dare hope there was a bright future ahead of him?

With the police needing to close the building site and put up cordons, there would be no work for a while, therefore, no fifty quid, but at least he'd been fed. He wouldn't need to worry about food now for a couple of days.

When a copper told him he could go, he wandered off the site and headed towards Mum's—he'd nick her hairdryer and straighteners, maybe some of that fancy makeup she used. He'd get enough for a small baggie of weed, at least.

He sighed, hating himself and wishing he had the guts to pull the plug on his own life, to die so Mum didn't have to worry anymore—there'd be no shame of having a junkie for a son, then. But the part of him with ambition and a zest for a decent life still nestled inside him somewhere, and so long as that voice kept chirping up every now and then, Ezra would plod on. But once it didn't speak anymore, it'd be game over.

The bones belonged to some woman Mum had worked with, one of those bloody awful slags who stood on street corners and flashed their legs and tits at passing motorists. Jodie Swain had worked at the Bordello but had got hooked on coke which had sent her out onto the streets to earn extra money to fund her habit. Of course, Mum had taken the opportunity to harp on about addiction and how it sent you down roads you shouldn't go down. He'd thought the same himself when it had hit the news as to who the woman was, her story unfolding online, and him, in one of his pondering moments, had felt sorry for her. He didn't need the pitfalls pointing out, but Mum wasn't to know that.

That was the thing with him, he thought a lot but didn't say a lot. He wanted to take action but never did—or he took the wrong action. He knew what was right and wrong but did the wrong thing anyway.

"Did you read about it? She was there for eight years under the ground," Mum said as they stood outside the Orange Lantern at half five in the morning, the sky lightening with the dawn. "We all knew something had happened to her back then, but the police wouldn't listen. Just like someone not a million miles from here won't listen either."

He rolled his eyes, making sure she saw it. "Can you skip the lecture and give me some money?"

"No. I'm not giving it to you anymore."

"You always say that, and then next time I come here you hand it over. You'll make up your mind one day."

"I mean it this time. I haven't been fair to you, chopping and changing things. You need a stable answer every time, and it's going to be no. I'm that worried you'll *end up under the ground one day, a*

drug deal gone wrong, and it'll be eight years before your body's found."

"You're being dramatic." But he'd worried about that himself, too. *"If you're not going to help, then just know if I* do *end up in a grave later today, it'll be your fault."*

That was his lowest blow yet, his cruellest emotional manipulation and, soaking up the hurt in her eyes, he then turned and walked away, waiting for her to call him back and say she had two hundred quid for him really, but she didn't.

Fuck it.

Chapter Twenty-Two

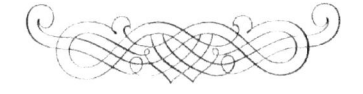

The day had dawned crisp and bright, frost stiffening the grass, warm breaths turning to clouds with every exhalation. The setting out of tables on the large expanses of grass either side of the church with the trees as a backdrop had been carried out by several volunteers, and those who'd booked a table to sell their crafts and whatnot had arrived to set up. A marquee had been erected, again with tables, and later the food would be laid out. Father Donovan already had five large boiled water dispensers heating up since early on, ready for the cups of tea, coffee, and hot chocolate. He looked forward to a happy day, a coming together of residents that would remind him of the year he'd first become a priest, when religion had been an important part of life. It seemed nowadays it had been cast aside—and also cast in a bad light. He aimed to change that.

A few local businesses had market stalls, plus fairground equipment had been set up in the field adjacent to the church. A swinging pirate ship, a carousel, and some waltzers. Someone had also brought a bungee jump thing, although to Michael it looked like kids would be boinging up and down on a trampoline with ropes attached to them. St John's Ambulance would be on hand, although he hoped the only issue anyone had was heartburn from the burger van, there for those who didn't fancy the free buffet on offer. Michael hoped it would be a big turnout, but most of all, he wanted to see lots of smiles and hear laughter. Life was too sombre these days for many, and a little levity and happiness would go a long way.

A distant scream drew his attention to the trees at the bottom of the park to the left, the ones that had a path through them leading to the housing estate. A woman—he couldn't make out her features from this distance—came running over the grass, and on instinct, Michael ran towards her, his heart hammering. They slowed at the point where they'd have clashed had they kept going, the woman bending over with her hands on her knees, air sawing in and out of her in angry-sounding wheezes. A voice popped up somewhere in the chaos of Michael's frantic mind and told him he needed to become fitter—his lungs had gone tight. He fired back that his job didn't exactly require him to be able to sprint but he'd take the warning on board and sort himself out.

He caught his breath and laid a hand on the woman's upper arm. "What's the matter?"

She stood upright, revealing her face. Fifty-something Miss Marchant (who looked more like seventy) was an avid supporter of Our Lady and had volunteered her services today to chat to residents and encourage them to spend money. She popped into the church most days, mainly with her feather duster to swipe it over the pews, regardless of the fact that Michael employed a cleaner.

"There's a…there's a…a body," she managed to get out and turned to point towards the trees. "I swear to God it's Jason. You know, Jason Ludlow."

Michael frowned, his brain not catching up with her words for a moment. He digested them, and his stomach rolled over. "What do you *mean*, a body?"

"He's not breathing. I watched his chest and it didn't go up and down. There's blood…"

Michael's first impulse was to phone the police, but he had to remind himself, yet again, that his priorities had changed. "You go on into the marquee and get yourself a cup of tea. The water should be hot enough now. I'll…I'll go and see Jason."

On his way over, he took his phone out and sent a quick message.

MICHAEL: ON WAY TO TREES IN PARK OPPOSITE CHURCH. PARISHIONER FOUND BODY. JASON LUDLOW. WHAT SHOULD I DO?

GG: POLICE AND AMBULANCE.

MICHAEL: OKAY.

Thankful he could go down the usual route, Michael reached the body and established Jason was dead, then dialled 999. He waited with the poor lad until paramedics and a couple of uniformed officers arrived.

Two detectives had shown up, too, one of them the nice Colin who worked for the twins, and Michael had to pretend he hadn't met him before when they'd introduced themselves.

"Um, do you think the fayre will have to be cancelled?" Michael asked.

Colin looked at his colleague. Nigel, was it?

Nigel shook his head. "These trees are so far away from the church that I'd say it was all right to continue. A cordon will go up along the pavement, preventing anyone from using the park. I'll apologise in advance, but there will obviously be a lot of police presence, and considering which Estate we live on, it may prevent certain people from attending your event."

Michael supposed it was the detective's polite way of saying the Cardigan Estate had a bad element that where Our Lady was based meant a lot of that element was local to the church. "That can only be a good thing, then, keeping the rowdier ones away. Feel free to come over in an hour or two. Once the buffet has been set up, you're welcome to a plate of food. We have hot and cold drinks."

"Any Pepsi Max?" Colin asked.

"We have cans of that, yes."

Colin appeared happy about that.

Michael hesitated to ask, as he thought his request would be denied, but he'd give it a go anyway. "Can I call Jason's grandmother? Kathleen Ludlow."

"I take it that's his next of kin," Nigel said.

"Yes, he's lived with his gran for years." Michael gave them the address.

"We'll pop round there in a bit," Colin said, "so we can deliver the sad news, but we'll tell her to give you a bell if you like. She may well need some support—some people don't like having family liaison officers in their space."

"Is there anything you can tell us about Jason?" Nigel stared over at the body and where officers in white outfits put up a tent of sorts around it.

"He's neurodiverse. I don't know what his diagnosis was, exactly, but he was fond of Our Lady, he'd have been there all the time if he could. His grandmother phoned me last night actually. Jason had a habit of hanging around the park every evening until eleven, watching the church to make sure nothing happened to it. Last night he witnessed the theft of flatscreen televisions that had been kindly donated for today's raffle. Two men had come in a white Transit. From what I can gather, Jason scared them by being there. One of them ran off towards the trees here, and the other drove off in the van. Jason had gone home and told Kathleen about it, and she then let me know."

"Did you report the robbery to the police?" Nigel enquired.

Colin gave Michael a slight head shake, likely to tell him not to mention the twins being told, as if he even would.

"I didn't. Because of how Jason was, I felt it would be too traumatising for him to be asked all those questions. I informed the donators of what had happened, and they'll be replacing the TVs today."

"That's good of them," Nigel said. "The type who have money to burn, are they?"

Michael just smiled. "What bothers me is that Jason looks like he's been on the ground there for a while. The blood on his neck isn't fresh. I have a horrible feeling that despite him going to bed, he must have got up again to come out here and watch the church. What if the thieves came back, too, and this is the result?" He waved an arm towards the tent. "Oh, and the thieves must have used lock picks, as no doors were damaged."

"Thank you for letting us know," Colin said.

Michael left them to it, and on the way back to the church, he informed the twins that he'd had to let the police know about the robbery. He added that Colin was one of the police officers on the scene.

MICHAEL: I DIDN'T TELL THEM WHO DONATED THE TELEVISIONS.

GG: IT WOULDN'T MATTER IF YOU DID. TOO MANY OF THE RESIDENTS KNOW, AND WORD WOULD GET BACK TO THEM ANYWAY, BUT THANKS FOR BEING CAUTIOUS. SEE YOU LATER.

The day was tainted now, but Michael would stick on a smile and continue as usual. There would be those curious to know what was going on, what with the cordon and the police being around, who would likely grab the chance to speak to people at the fayre to see if they could gather any information. It could be as Michael had suggested, though—the thieves had come back, and they'd killed Jason to keep him quiet, which didn't make sense as their faces had been covered.

So had someone else killed him?

Pulled out of his thoughts at the sight of Miss Marchant coming over, he prepared himself to hear what she'd told the police.

"I'm that shaken up," she said. "It was such a shock to find him like that."

Michael made all the right soothing noises, and perhaps uncharitably, he imagined she'd dine out on this story for months to come. She liked a bit of a gossip, and he had no doubt she'd enjoy being the star of the show. "Absolutely terrible, Miss Marchant. I can relate to how upsetting it was as I saw him for myself."

"He was stabbed in the neck." She shuddered.

He smiled to stop himself from shaking his head—she also liked to state the obvious. "Did the police tell you not to contact Kathleen?"

"Yes, but it'll be difficult to hold myself back."

"Please let them do their job. There's time enough for us to help her grieve after the news has sunk in."

It was a gentle warning so she didn't go running round to Kathleen's house and blurt the news in that awful way she usually did. Miss Marchant didn't understand the word tact.

"Do you need to go home?" he asked. "I can imagine you're traumatised and understandably may not want to face the public today."

"Oh no," she said. "I'd prefer to be around people. I don't want to be alone with my thoughts and that *ghastly* image in my head."

You want to tell everyone what's happened, that's what you want.

Michael smiled and nodded. A couple of women had already caught wind of Miss Marchant being the one to have discovered the body, so he walked away as they approached her. Yes, she was going to hold court all day.

A white Transit drew up, and Micheal stiffened. Were those robbers back? A man with a clipboard got out and headed for Michael, jerking his head as if to tell him he needed to talk in private. Nervous, Michael led the way to a secluded cluster of trees, the graveyard visible between the trunks.

What am I doing? He could be anyone…

No, it'll be okay. There are too many people around.

"Can I help you?" Michael darted his gaze over the man's shoulder and gave a wave—at no one, but he didn't want him thinking he could get away with... *Get away with what? Killing you? You're paranoid.*

"The twins told me I have to stay with the new tellies until they've been won." The man cuffed the end of his nose with his sleeve. "So is there anywhere I can park the van out of the way?"

Relieved, Michael instructed him where to go, then he got on with overseeing the fayre preparations. For the majority of the time it took his mind away from the awful murder, but every so often in an idle moment, the sight of Jason Ludlow's dead body filled his mind's eye and he had to take a minute to compose himself.

Michael felt he had to take some blame for the death. If he hadn't agreed to the television donation, they wouldn't have been stolen and Jason would still be alive.

I really need to go to confession about that...

Chapter Twenty-Three

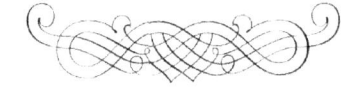

The Grey Suits pub was basically a business model replica of the Noodle. Cheap, decent food, free coffee refills after paying for the first cup, and somewhere nice to spend some time that made the punters think they were in a gastropub and a step up the social ladder. All of it for a fair price, not too hard on the pocket—unless they wanted alcoholic drinks. The food was the draw, and people tended to hang around for 'just one more' when it came to pints, shots, and shorts.

Kenny and Liz Feldon had taken to training really well. Nessa from the Noodle had been here for a week to show them the ropes, and the couple had come on in leaps and bounds as though born to be publicans. The shadow of grief still shrouded them, that much was obvious, their only son killed by that Precious bitch, all because he'd pulled his phone out to video her shooting someone else. Liz often muttered that if her boy hadn't been skiving school, he'd still be alive today, and Kenny always told her that you couldn't change fate no matter how hard you tried. Still, they smiled and laughed to hide the pain, and even if they were only *pretending* to live their lives to the fullest, they certainly had customers fooled into thinking they were genuinely happy. It would be their first Christmas without the lad, but George reckoned the pub being so busy and all the parties they'd planned for the festive season would hopefully keep their minds off their mourning.

George and Greg had opted for a fry-up and a coffee. While their food was being cooked, they'd have a chat with Kenny and Liz in the office. Liz sat behind the desk as if pleased to rest her feet, and Kenny leaned against the wall beside a filing cabinet. George and Greg sat in the two chairs on the other side of the desk.

"Is everything all right?" Kenny asked.

"With you two, yes, it's perfect. We're here to ask if you noticed some bloke called Marcus Rupert in here banging on about selling flatscreen televisions." Intel had come in overnight, and George had a picture of Marcus on their work burner. He brought it up on the screen and turned it so Kenny could have a look. Then he showed Liz.

She nodded. "I'm sure he was in a few nights ago, going from table to table and bending, talking quietly." She glanced at her husband. "Do you remember? You went over and asked him what he was up to, and he made out he was friends with everyone he spoke to."

Kenny pinched the skin beneath his nose. "Yeah. He went and sat down at a table by himself after that, but a couple of the blokes he'd nattered to went over to him. So are you saying he was flogging televisions right under our noses?"

"The televisions that were stolen from the church. The ones we donated for the Christmas fayre." George scowled. "It fucking pissed me right off. We're letting the recipients of the televisions have them. They were bought by husbands for their wives. I didn't want the women to be upset when they didn't get what they asked Santa for."

"Or Marcus, in this case," Greg said. "Have you seen him in here since then?"

Kenny shook his head. "I take it you want us to let you know if he does come in?"

"Yeah," George said, "but hopefully we'll have rounded him up today. I was thinking of doing it before the Christmas fayre, but to be honest with you, he doesn't look like he's going anywhere. The bloke who's watching him says he's gone home, so maybe he's spending the day indoors. He's probably naffed off because the bloke he usually uses to deliver the stolen goods for him has handed in his notice, so to speak. He's going to be working for us. His name's Alexander Moody. Have you heard of him?"

"Should we have?" Liz bit her lip as if she was worried Moody's name had been mentioned before and she'd since forgotten it. "Sorry, but we've been learning so much lately, my mind's full…"

"It was a general query. We've had him checked out and he's clean as far as we're aware, but we have people out there asking questions about him. If you hear his name mentioned in here, let us know."

Kenny pushed off the wall and ran both hands through his hair. "Do you think we'll get any through traffic because of the fayre?"

"I should imagine you'll get a few people in come the evening. We've only laid on a lunch buffet, and if everyone stays at the fayre until late, they're going to be hungry. Is there anything you needed to discuss before we shoot off to eat our grub?"

"No, all's good here," Kenny said. "We always go to Nessa if we have any queries. She's been so bloody helpful and kind—I thought you should know that."

George appreciated being told. It stood to reason that Nessa was fucking brilliant at what she did, otherwise they wouldn't employ her, but it didn't hurt for them to tell her every now and again. She was so competent that George tended to forget and left her to it. He'd get some flowers sent round to the Noodle with a note telling her to take a spa day on the house. Yes, she got paid a fair whack to run their pub, but appreciating someone and showing it went a long way, and she'd be well chuffed at getting a pamper day off.

"We'll give her a little treat," George said, "but don't tell her because I'd like it to be a surprise. Actually, talking of treats… Once the Christmas rush is over, I want you two off on holiday. We're paying for it and will arrange managerial cover for when you're away—Nessa can do it while her staff run the Noodle."

"We don't need a holiday," Liz said.

"I disagree." George smiled at her. "Pick somewhere in the world where your son would have wanted to go."

"Disneyland," Kenny said.

"Then you'll go there—for him." George stood and left the room before things got too sentimental. Liz's sob chased him out, and he filled his coffee cup then smiled at the waitress coming over with both of their breakfasts.

Greg sat beside him. "Thanks for leaving me with a crying husband and wife, you knob."

"You're welcome."

"That was a lovely thing you did."

"It's been known. Got to do nice shit to level out the bad."

Greg tutted. "Don't tell me you've got a guilty conscience about Kash."

"Nope, but we see so many arseholes that when we come into contact with good people, it makes me want to do good things. Those two have put aside their grief to get this place up and running for us, and even though it's only been a few months, they deserve a break already."

"I agree, but then Nessa deserves a break, too. Look at how she's trained them and how you automatically chose her to take over running this place when those two swan off on holiday."

"I'd already decided to send her flowers and a voucher for a spa day."

"Then send her a holiday voucher an' all, say she can go after the Feldons get back from theirs."

George nodded, gestured to his breakfast to tell his brother to shut the fuck up now, and got on with eating. He thought about all of their other core staff, how they hadn't been rewarded either with free holidays and whatnot. Once this shit with Marcus was over and done with, he'd sit down and work out a schedule for everyone to have time off. He couldn't expect tip-top work from staff who poured from empty teapots.

Chapter Twenty-Four

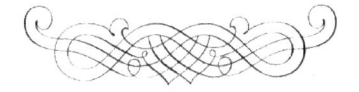

Colin and Nigel had been to see Kathleen Ludlow earlier, and Colin couldn't stop thinking about her, how broken she'd been at the news of Jason's death. It seemed the lad had been her only reason for living, as all the life whooshed out of her when it sank in that he wasn't coming home. The burning urge to find whoever had killed her grandson continued to boil inside him as if it were his own family member he needed to find justice for—all the poor bastard had wanted to do was protect Our Lady, and he'd paid for it with his life.

They were going back to the crime scene having changed into casual clothes rather than staying in their usual suits. Nigel wanted them to pretend to be people going to the fayre—with any luck, the killer might come back. Nigel planned to take a lot of photographs, and one of the forensic lot would be there doing the same under the guise of being there for the local newspaper. Janine was taking Rosie in her pushchair to give the baby some fresh air, so Colin looked forward to seeing the little one he'd grown so fond of.

"Some news has come in," Nigel said as they got into the car at the station. "I didn't want to tell you in the office; there's too many people about."

Colin stuck his seat belt on. This must be to do with his wife's case, otherwise Nigel would have said it in front of the others. "Go on…" There wasn't much else he could say. Well, there was, like, "Wait a minute, I'm not ready," and "Shit, have you found who it is?" and "Don't talk yet, I don't think I can take any more…"

Nigel pulled out of the car park. "Um, Erin has found something pretty fucking significant on the one hand, but on the other, it might not be."

He doesn't want me to get my hopes up. "Spit it out."

"First off, I never know which name to use for your wife, her birth one or the one she changed it to."

"The one she changed it to. She hated the other one."

"Okay. The fibres found around Libby's neck, the ones that matched her scarf, are also a match for fibres found when builders discovered bones not too long ago. The crime scene is now a housing estate called Blue Monk."

Colin's stomach rolled over. He recalled the case—Janine had a habit of bringing past ones up to fill dips in conversation. "Jodie Swain."

"Yes. Those fibres were also from a scarf—exclusive to Fusion Fashions, popular at the time of sale. The shop sold handmade goods, and the owner had created the wool blend herself. You said Libby had hers for many years, so it makes sense in Jodie's timeline, too, as in Libby would have bought hers around the time of Jodie's death."

"So either Jodie and Libby happened to have the same scarf, or the killer chose them *because* they had the red scarves, or... Either way, there was no DNA anywhere near Jodie's bones other than her own, I remember Janine telling me about it, so if it's the same killer, he's clever enough not to leave anything behind, as we've discovered already."

"I just wanted you to know, even if it turns out to be a dead end."

"Thanks, but it brings more questions than answers. Like why was Jodie killed, likely raped, and buried in a field that years later turned out to be a building site, when my wife was raped and murdered in her own home and left in situ. Jodie was a sex worker, Libby wasn't."

"Maybe the scarf was literally the only link. Erin previously did a database search on red fibres when the bones were found. A few came up, two of them definite matches for the Fusion Fashions scarves—and they also matched the ones in Jodie's case."

"So a serial killer," Colin said. "Can I ask... Why is it only coming to light about the fibres now? It's been a while since Libby died." Died, as if it was a *normal* thing. "Since she was *killed*."

"Forensic backlog."

It wasn't unheard of for results to come back weeks or months down the line, but… Colin shrugged, affecting nonchalance. "No one's fault, it's just the way it is, but at least we're getting somewhere. We now know all of the linked women owned a Fusion Fashions scarf. He could be one of those pervy types who watched the women buying them, then he followed them home."

Nigel frowned. "But Libby's scarf was bought years ago. Why did he wait to kill her?" He slapped his forehead. "Unless he was put in the nick for something else, or moved elsewhere in the country or abroad."

"My thoughts exactly. Fucking creepy that he must have either memorised or written down our address… And he must have been watching our house to make sure *we* hadn't moved and it was the same woman." The idea of that gouged a hole in Colin's psyche. He was a copper, he should have twigged someone was watching them.

Unless he knows I'm a copper and only watched her while I was at work.

Part of him wished it had been as they'd previously thought—a random rape/murder, nothing more. Now, with the knowledge it had been so much more than that…planned, all four fibre women chosen, and his poor missus had been living on borrowed time until her killer could get to her…

Tears stung, and he stared out of the passenger window to hide from Nigel as they overspilled and rolled down his cheeks. "It's all a bit shit really." What a silly thing to say, but he had no other words.

"We'll get him, Col, I promise."

"Never promise, because in our line of work, we can never guarantee a result."

"Yeah, well, you know what I meant."

The rest of the journey was spent in silence save for Colin's occasional sniff. Nigel got lucky and nabbed a parking spot in the long line of cars snaking down the road outside the church. They got out, and Colin spotted Janine immediately — her bright-pink coat gave her away. So he and Nigel didn't look conspicuous, he broke away from his boss, as they'd planned, and headed for Janine, eager to tell her about the red fibres. She stood by a candyfloss stall eating a bag of marshmallows which she then stuffed in her bag hanging on the pram handles.

"All right, Col?"

He didn't nod—she'd know he was lying if he did—but bent over to peer inside the confines of the pushchair where Rosie was bundled up warm in a cocoon of blankets. She slept, her dummy moving in and out as she sucked it.

"Out with it," Janine said.

Colin told her.

She let out a long breath. "It could have been that he was in prison, the reason why he didn't go after Libby for so long. We did factor that in, I remember saying it to the team. Jodie was estimated to be under the ground for eight years, which matched when she went missing, and another two years have passed since then, so if prison is the reason, it was a ten-year stretch, and the same goes for if he moved away."

"Yes, and he could have carried on killing elsewhere. I'll mention that to Nigel."

"Erin will look into it. She's great with things like that."

Colin didn't doubt it. "I find it fucking creepy, if it *is* the same bloke, that he remembered Libby and went back for her all these years later." He mentioned about how the man could have watched her, and the others, buying those scarves from the little boutique. "We won't get lucky and find CCTV after all that time, and the shop's shut down now."

"I reckon it'll be old-fashioned police work that finds him," Janine said. "It could take years, but on the other hand, he could slip up, kill someone else, and leave DNA behind this time. So long as the fibres are present, it's a good chance it's the same man."

Colin didn't want to think about this, let alone say it out loud, but he had to. "I wonder if he made Libby go and get her scarf out of the cupboard under the stairs. It was warm when she died, summer, remember? She wouldn't have had the scarf out on the coat rack. So he was confident enough about spending time in our house for her to look for it. What an arrogant bastard."

"You knew he wasn't pushed for time anyway, based on the crime scene, but this confirms it. I agree, she must have collected the scarf for it to have been tied around her neck, likely during the sexual assault, but as you said, it was put back in the cupboard afterwards, and only the fibres left an indication as to what he'd used. I'm so sorry, Col."

He nodded and looked around—he was here to do a job, not gossip, but it'd been so good to get it off his chest. Janine pushed the buggy in between people, and with no more words to be said for now, Colin watched everybody, as did Janine. Once a copper, always a copper.

They'd done two laps of the area when she said, "Not one person looks suspicious. If anything, they look worried."

It took a moment to switch his mind away from Libby and to the subject Janine was on about—Jason Ludlow's killer. "I thought the same. It's like they want to be here to have a bit of fun, but at the same time they're wondering if they're safe. For all we know, the killer could be here and is either good at hiding any anxiety or really doesn't give a toss about what they've done. It's incredibly difficult for me to pretend not to be a copper as well. I keep thinking I'm standing out like a sore thumb."

He wasn't going to tell her that he viewed every man of a certain age here as his wife's killer. A couple of people had red scarves on, and it had taken a great amount of strength to inspect them without making it too obvious as to what he was doing. Thankfully, they both had the appearance of being tightly woven, whereas Libby's had been more loosely woven and looked hand-knitted.

Still, it didn't stop the rush of paranoia that the killer would choose those two women next. He wanted to tell them to take the scarves off, but he'd come off as a complete nutter, and considering he knew damn well the scarves of the deceased were from a particular shop and had a certain style, nothing like those two, he really needed to get a grip.

Maybe Nigel shouldn't have told me anything until the end of the day.

But then Colin had told Nigel to inform him as soon as anything came in, so he only had himself to blame for how he was feeling now. Going by the timeline, including the deaths of the other two women, he imagined the age of the killer. He could still be classed as young. Or he could be an old man now, grey hair, wrinkles beside his eyes. Maybe that was why Libby had felt safe when he'd knocked on the door—assuming he'd even done that as no neighbours had seen anything of significance. Colin suspected the man had come down the side of the house when Libby was sitting at the patio table drinking a coffee.

The not knowing was doing his head in.

"I doubt you'll ever know the truth," Janine said as if she'd read his mind. "You'll always be tormented by it: did she do this, did she do that? The crime scene tells only part of the story, doesn't it?"

He nodded. "We can usually fill in the puzzle pieces by ourselves, but sometimes there are a couple of bits missing where we don't quite know what went on. Like I said to Nigel, my missus was killed at home and left there on the hallway floor, but Jodie was killed in what had once been a field and buried. What about the others?"

"They were also dumped in fields."

"So Libby having that scarf might be a massive coincidence if the MO isn't the same."

"Also, only Jodie was a sex worker. The other two…one was a cashier, the other an admin assistant."

"So it really is likely that he watched for the women buying the scarves and went from there. What the fuck has a red scarf got to do with anything in his past, because you can guarantee it'll be there somewhere."

"Maybe his mother owned one. His grandmother, his sister, his aunt. They could have bought it around the same time as the other women did. Who knows, it could be a woman he fancied and he asked her out and she told him to get lost; he became fixated on the scarf she was wearing at the time or one she bought shortly afterwards—and he knew that because he possibly stalked her. You know how it goes, how their minds work."

"I wonder if Nigel would do an appeal on the red scarf? Any women who own one, ask them to come forward."

"It's not a bad shout, actually. Send him a message about it now so you don't forget. Maybe that's why he told you about the fibres, so while you were walking around here your brain percolated. Us DIs do have a method to our madness, you know."

"He more than likely knew I'd tell you, and you'd come up with a theory or angle."

Colin took his phone out and sent his thoughts to Nigel, plus a suggestion that all ten-year prison sentences—or thereabouts—could be looked into from when Jodie was killed. Even if it was just a press release in all the newspapers about the scarf it would be enough, it didn't have to be a conference on the telly. But if this man had a ten-year break because he'd been *unable* to kill, all of his frustrations would be bubbling by now, ready to be released. He'd killed Colin's wife and may at this very moment be reacquainting himself with his next victim.

Colin wanted to scream at the thought.

Chapter Twenty-Five

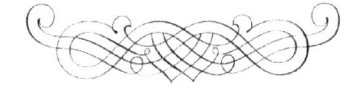

The police presence at the fayre was unavoidable, considering some poor bastard had been murdered by the trees. Still, George and Greg hadn't had a hand in that, so it wasn't like they had to feel guilty, was it. Nevertheless, with coppers over the road from Our Lady, Colin, Janine, Nigel, and fuck knows who else prowling the crowds, George reckoned they ought to watch what they said and did while here. Whether he could do that was another matter. He had a tendency to act now, think later.

It wasn't often they were present at public events where they could be under scrutiny from many pairs of eyes. All right, they did their weekly appearance at Jackpot Palace, and they were regulars at the Noodle and now The Grey Suits, but there were unknown variables here, and the fact they'd had to leave their guns in the BMW was a tad disconcerting. They had their bulletproof vests on, as usual, and not many people knew they wore them, so any attempt at attacking their chests and backs would prove pointless. But would anyone risk that when so many police were around?

George hadn't expected to feel so vulnerable, so open and exposed. Had the police not been here, he would have gadded about as though he owned the place, his usual confidence exuded over the masses so they knew who was boss. He'd given Colin and Janine a nod and walked on as if he didn't know them, which was difficult because he wanted to talk to Colin about Jason's murder. There was the gran to go and see as well, give her their condolences and some money for the funeral. There was Marcus to round up, too, so all in all, they wouldn't exactly be staying here for long anyway. Too much to do.

On their previous visits to Our Lady, George and Greg had made no secret of the fact they were donating funds to support the church, so walking up to Father Donovan wouldn't be seen as odd. The priest tilted his head in a gesture that indicated they should move to one side to talk. George and Greg followed him towards a van George recognised as one of theirs, the driver also one of theirs.

"People are going to clam up with you here," Michael said. "They're not going to want to talk freely, not just about the murder but about anything if they know you're hanging around. I appreciate you had to show your faces, especially given what happened across the road, potentially making it look rather obvious you may possibly be here in search of the killer instead of being here to talk about the benefits of grassing with your residents."

"I thought much the same," Greg said.

George nodded. "But if we hadn't come, it might have looked like *we* killed Jason. Have you heard anything new on that by the way? Our copper hasn't been in touch for a while."

"I've got a feeling a lot of them are plainclothes, clearly acting like they've just come to the fayre."

"That wouldn't be unusual. Maybe the police think that with a murder happening so close to the church, albeit many metres away across the road, that the killer might come back to witness the upset they've caused."

"Do you think one of the robbers came back and waited for him?" Michael glanced around, whittling his fingers. "Jason didn't see their faces, so I don't understand why that would have happened."

"The robbery clearly upset the lad and he came back to check on the church. I've had word from our man who was sitting outside. He spoke to Jason and told him to go home. He watched him walk towards the trees. Whoever killed him was waiting in there. Maybe they saw our man and stayed hidden, then struck when Jason came along."

"He was stabbed in the shoulder and neck." Michael shuddered. "The thought of him lying there for hours before Miss Marchant found him…"

"Who's Miss Marchant?"

Michael pointed to a woman who appeared to be in her sixties or seventies. "She always comes to the church via the trees. She lives on the estate over there. Unfortunately, she's now living it up as though she's famous because everyone wants to ask her about the discovery of the body."

"That's a bit fucking distasteful," George said and strode towards the woman who held court in front of two others. He stared at the extras in this pantomime until they skuttled away, glancing at him over their shoulders. "I hear you've been lording it up as if you're some kind of celebrity."

Miss Marchant visibly shivered and linked her fingers together. "I was only passing on what I saw this morning, that's all. There's no crime in that."

"There is when you're acting like it's an episode of *EastEnders* and not real life."

"I was telling my side of the story."

She was a stubborn cow, and George had had enough of her already. He leaned forward to whisper in her ear, "Why don't you suddenly get a headache and fuck off home? You're not welcome here spreading your bullshit." He pulled back to peer at her expression in order to gauge her response to his words.

She raised her eyebrows. "Why don't *you* suddenly fuck off home? We did well enough without your presence at other fetes and whatnot. Why are you even here? You've never been bothered about our church until recently, so what are you playing at? What's your aim? Why are you trying to butter up Father Donovan?"

George had had a chat with Greg recently about granny bashing, and this was the first time he *truly* wanted to punch an older woman in the face. Her arrogance was staggering—she was the type who didn't feel a leader's rules applied to her and that if she wanted to say something, it was her right, *because* of her age. She thought she'd get away with being rude.

He cocked his head at her. "You'll keep."

At last she appeared uneasy, unsure of how to retaliate. "You really ought to watch what you say to people when there are so many police officers around." She glanced about as if ready to call one of them over, a return serve to what he'd volleyed at her, a little threat of her own that bothered him not one bit.

He smiled a fake smile. "You really want to watch how you talk to me, but that's a story for another day. Like I said, you'll keep."

He walked away from her, back to Michael and Greg who discussed whether it would be easier to pick the names out of the hat for the televisions now or later.

"Later," Greg said. "That way people will hang around and spend money at the stalls, which is what you wanted so you could raise money."

"I'm worried about your man sitting in that van all day."

George eyed Miss Marchant who'd wandered away to speak to some old fella, probably telling him all about their little interaction. "Don't worry about him, he's paid to sit there. Does Miss Marchant have any family?"

Michael frowned. "She has a niece who lives somewhere abroad. Crete, I think. Why do you ask?"

George put his lying mask on. "I'm conscious that she's had a traumatic experience this morning, and if she lives alone, she might feel vulnerable when it gets dark. What's her address? I'll send someone to persuade her to let us put up security cameras, in case the killer finds out she was the one who discovered the body and phoned the police, then subsequently gossiped about it all day. Murderers can get a bit funny about that sort of thing and they might retaliate."

"Good grief, that's an awful thought." Michael recited her address from a notes app in his phone.

Now George had set up the reason for Miss Marchant being found with a bruise or two come tomorrow (because Ruffian was going to sneak out and administer them during the night), he changed the subject. "Well, I think we've shown our faces here for long enough. I honestly feel our presence is a hindrance rather than a help. It's obvious people aren't relaxing with us around, so we'll leave you be. We'll nip and see the gran. What's her name again?"

"Kathleen Ludlow." Michael told him her address, too. "Shall I let Miss Marchant know someone will be calling round later?"

"Yeah." George would arrange for Cameron to pop there and put cameras up, but not until after Ruffian had been. "Tell her it'll be tomorrow. Hopefully it'll put her mind at rest."

He moved through the crowd, dodging kids who darted here and there, their faces sticky from candyfloss, which prompted a memory from his childhood when they'd been to a funfair and how, on the outside, he and Greg used to go around as if they didn't have a care in the world, but the minute they stepped through the front door and Richard raised his hand or shouted, any happiness they'd felt at being free on the dodgems suddenly vanished. He hoped these sticky-faced children didn't suffer the same thing behind closed doors.

He made eye contact with Janine and then shifted his sights to the buggy to let her know he was asking if Rosie was okay. Janine lifted a thumb from the handle of the pushchair in answer, and she turned to the hook-a-duck stall. George took his phone out and held it up as if taking a selfie when he spotted Colin to get the point across that he needed an update. He supposed if the copper hadn't got in contact yet there was nothing to report, but then again, Colin was the type to ponder things before he got in touch. He was conscious that what he had to say had to be important enough to bother them with. Colin discreetly nodded and walked to the food marquee. He'd probably gone in there for one of his beloved cans of Pepsi Max.

George sensed his brother right behind him, so he left the churchyard and crossed the road, walking down the pavement alongside the police cordon. A couple of young PCs stared at them in awe, at least that's what their expressions seemed to convey, but George ignored them and continued down the path towards the BMW, which they'd parked a fair way down the long line of vehicles.

In the car, he took out a packet of Tangfastics, something he hadn't eaten in a while, and chewed on them as Greg drove away. "Just so you know, I'm going to be teaching Miss Marchant a lesson."

Greg glanced across at him and frowned. "Why, what's she done?"

"I don't like her attitude. She had no respect for me whatsoever." George explained, feeling justified in his decision. "It was like she thought it was okay to make herself the star of the story instead of actually having sympathy for Jason and his gran. It pissed me off."

"So what are you going to do to her?"

"Go in as Ruffian in the middle of the night. Shit her up a bit. Make out I'm Jason's killer and

I've come for her. Warn her to stop talking about it."

"Are you going to hit her?"

"She'll have to have some bruises, yes, but if you're going to get funny about me punching an old lady—"

"She isn't actually old, she just dresses and looks like it. Michael reckons she's only fifty-something."

George felt better about that. "Then I won't be granny bashing, will I? Maybe I'll clamp my hand around her throat, create bruises that way."

"I'll come." Greg sighed. "I'll be your getaway driver. You know I don't like you going out on your own as Ruffian." He took a right turn into Kathleen's street. "But if you're only going after Miss Marchant because your pride's been dented, then you need to rethink your plans."

George would admit it was a knee-jerk reaction to make the decision to go round to her house, but God knows how many people she'd spoken to today, glorifying the murder, and he had no doubt she'd continue to do so until the final person had left the fayre. She'd wring out every last bit of attention, he was sure of it.

"Whatever." He took their burner out of his pocket. It had vibrated, and he was eager to see if Colin had made contact.

He had. George read an update about Libby's murder: Red fibres from a Fusion Fashions scarf that were the same as three other women whose bodies had been found years ago. It seemed the killer had taken a decade off—by choice or forced?—and then started up again. Months had passed since Colin's missus had died, so maybe she'd been the final one and it would stop now. But what if it didn't? What if there were other red-scarf ladies on his list? The idea of some of their residents who owned that same scarf, unknowingly victims until the killer made himself known, meant George was going to have to do something about it.

He explained what had gone on to Greg.

"A blanket message needs to go out to all Cardigan Crew employees to get the word out about that scarf," Greg said. "Anyone who owned—or still owns—that particular one in that particular colour from ten or more years ago needs to be vigilant and also contact the police."

George did that then let Colin know what he'd put into action.

Colin: Thank you. I expect Nigel will do the same thing, but it doesn't hurt to spread the word even more. I want this bastard caught.

GG: So do we. Any news about Jason? We're about to go and see his gran.

Colin: Nigel let me know that a witness came forward and saw someone leaving the trees and heading into the housing estate. Current status on that = Needle in a haystack.

GG: We'll do some investigating on our end. Talk to you soon.

Greg parked outside Kathleen's. "What's what?"

George passed on the info about the person in the trees. "With no CCTV on that estate bar outside the row of shops, the police will be relying on video doorbells and whatnot. I don't really think we ought to send anyone to poke around the part of the estate that's closest to the trees. With an active police investigation going on, residents are going to be more vigilant and maybe phone it in about suspicious people when really they're just our blokes asking questions. I'd rather send them into the couple of pubs on that estate and listen instead."

"We should ask Kash what he was doing. He could have gone back looking for Jason."

"It's going to be a bit difficult to speak to him at the moment, he's in hospital, but we can send one of our nurses in to talk to him while we chat to Kathleen."

George contacted her, pressed SEND, and got out of the car, bending and reaching back into the glove box to take out the thick funeral envelope. They walked up Kathleen's garden path, and he sensed eyes on them, neighbours on the lookout for the old woman—they'd know why the twins were paying a visit.

As he was about to knock on the door, the phone bleeped.

NURSE 3: HE SEEMS TO HAVE FORGOTTEN WHERE HE WAS.

George turned to Greg and told him what the text said.

Greg shook his head. "We'll pay him a visit when he's out of hospital. We'll wait until his parents have gone out."

The front door opened, cutting off their conversation, revealing an old woman who'd clearly been crying, her eyes and the end of her nose red. "I'd hoped you'd come, that my Jason was important enough for one of these visits."

George smiled. "Shall we go inside, love? I'll make you a nice cup of tea."

She turned and shuffled down the hallway, the picture of broken.

I'm going to kill the bastard who did this to her.

Chapter Twenty-Six

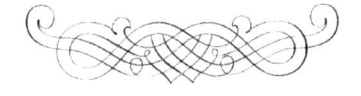

Marcus couldn't get over the fact that Moody had told him he wasn't available for work anymore. It was a cheek, that's what it was, calling the shots when it wasn't his place to do so. Moody was a bit of a thick bastard, only useful for picking up and delivering goods and acting like a menace if it was required. Marcus didn't think the man had much else about him, so his claim that he was moving on to a better job sounded like a load of bullshit.

That was the thing with people. You taught them all you knew and built them up from nothing, and it got them greedy, wanting more, then they ditched you without a by your leave, and you had to train someone all over again to do their job. Marcus had always had someone to do the grunt work, and he hadn't been best pleased having to deliver those televisions himself. The men who'd bought them had been so chuffed he'd followed through on his promise to supply them, and he'd even stuck around until they'd been plugged in to ensure they were in good working order.

You couldn't say fairer than that, could you.

This boded well for word of mouth to spread that Marcus was a man to be trusted, even though the goods came from questionable sources. Most people didn't give a shit *where* stuff had come from so long as they got it cheaper. He'd kept his ear to the ground this morning regarding the church robbery, and it seemed word hadn't got around about it. Not yet. Maybe Father Donovan was keeping it quiet, and as the twins had provided the televisions in the first place, they also might want to keep the theft secret. They wouldn't want anyone thinking they'd been done over, even if it had been indirectly.

He messaged Moody, as he had several times earlier, and expected to be ignored again, but three dots popped up where Moody was typing. It was the middle of the afternoon now, so maybe his former employee was sitting in the pub, two beers in, the alcohol prodding him to respond.

MOODY: OKAY, MEET ME IN THE GREY SUITS. IF YOU CAN GIVE ME BETTER WAGES THAN MY NEW BOSS, AND BETTER WORKING CONDITIONS, THEN MAYBE WE SHOULD TALK.

Marcus didn't like being told what was what, but on this occasion, as he had large a consignment of Minecraft toys to distribute before the Big Day, he could do with Moody coming back into the fold to do it for him.

MARCUS: ALL RIGHT. SEE YOU IN A BIT.

No need to sound too desperate, was there. 'In a bit' gave the impression Marcus wasn't that fussed, when in fact, he needed Moody back at work ASAP so was fussed as fuck.

He turned to look outside between the slats of his Venetian blind. The same car was out there from earlier, the one parked two doors down on the opposite side of the road. He'd noticed it when he'd come back from delivering the tellies, but this time there wasn't anyone in it.

He closed the blind, doing the same all around the house, plus shutting the curtains to boot. The afternoon had become dark quickly, and in another hour he reckoned there'd be complete blackness. In the hallway, he popped his coat and boots on, stuck a beanie over his wayward hair, and left the house.

The driver was back in the car.

Marcus stared over and contemplated going to ask what he was doing—waiting for someone? Watching someone? Him? Fuck, what if the twins had got wind that he'd organised the robbery and they'd sent someone to keep an eye on him? What if Moody had grassed him up? What if this trip to The Grey Suits was a lure, a trick?

Nah, Moody wouldn't do that to me.

Marcus got in his car and drove away, staring into the rearview mirror and waiting for the car to follow. It didn't, so he shrugged off his paranoia and went on his way, looking forward to a nice pint of Guinness and one of those tasty meals the pub put on the specials board—they were cheaper than those on the menu, and he was all about saving a bit of money.

Chapter Twenty-Seven

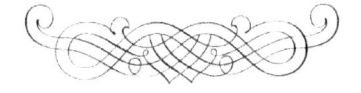

In disguise as down-on-their-luck drifters, George and Greg sat at the table behind Moody, having given him instructions on what to do and say when Marcus turned up. The man in question strolled in, taking off a beanie and stuffing it in his jacket pocket. He glanced around, spotted Moody, then approached the bar and placed an order. The man seemed calm enough to the casual observer, although the telltale darting of his eyes gave away the fact that he was on edge and trying to hide it.

"This bloke needs to up his fucking game," George whispered. "You can tell he's shitting himself from a mile away."

Greg ignored him, and Moody picked up his pint to hide a smile. Marcus used a card to pay and then brought his lager over and sat opposite Moody so George had a bird's-eye view of Marcus's face.

"What are you playing at?" Marcus sounded like he was joking, but it was obvious there was an underlying edge to his words, a dash of irritation lacing the vowels.

Moody picked up a beer mat and tapped it on the table. "I got made a better offer, it's as simple as that. Less hours, too, and as far as I'm aware, there's no robbing involved."

George coughed.

"Or if there *is* stealing," Moody went on, "then I doubt very much it'll be from a fucking church, and I can guarantee I won't be thieving anything from the twins like you did."

Good man, get him to confess.

"Keep your bloody voice down. I didn't do anything," Marcus whispered. "It was that fucking Kash and whoever else he roped into working with him. Listen, have you heard anything going round about that robbery? Some bloke's sitting outside my house in a car. All right, it might not be anything to do with me, but it's got me suspicious."

"What about?" Moody asked.

"You for a start. You could have dobbed me in to the twins, this meeting could be nothing but a trap."

"That doesn't sound right," Moody said. "I mean, you've always told me that I'm not clever enough to organise a piss-up in a brewery, so how would I have the brain cells to tell the twins that you arranged that robbery? I can't be clever and thick at the same time, can I?"

"All right, no need to get sarky. What's wrong with you anyway? You're never normally off with me, yet you've been rude a few times. You dropped those tellies off and then told me to stuff your job up my arse, you ignored all my messages, and then you asked me to come here and have been rude again. Do I need to remind you that my bully boys will fuck you over if I tell them about what you've done?"

"See, that's the funny thing." Moody sat back and got more comfortable. "I've never seen these bully boys of yours. This is how it usually goes down: You find out who to rob from, you find the people to do the robbery, then you use me to pick up the goods and store them in the lock-up, then it was me who delivered them. Some of the places I've been to for you have been well dodgy, yet not once did you send any of your bully-boy backup with me. I reckon it's all a load of bollocks."

Marcus looked like he wanted to explode. He slapped a hand on the beer mat to stop Moody from tapping it, then he snatched it away and scrunched it in his fist. Greg made a strangled sound, as though trying to stop himself from laughing at the show of anger, and George could understand why this seemed amusing, but he didn't find it funny. Marcus was playing at being a hardman, using his words to weave an illusion that he was much more protected than anyone thought and that a team of henchman would appear at any given moment if he clicked his fingers. George could see through the ruse. Marcus had lied to Moody, fabricating some gangster world they inhabited, when in fact, Marcus was nothing but a two-bit ponce who nicked a few things and sold them on. George was willing to bet the televisions were the biggest haul of his crappy little career so far.

He was finding it difficult to stay in place and not say something.

"I'll get them here now then, shall I?" Marcus took his phone out of his pocket and jabbed at the screen, maybe waiting for Moody to shout out for him to stop.

"Yeah, I'd like to meet them," Moody said. "See who I need to be wary of down a dark alley, because I've changed my mind. Even if you pay me extra and treat me better, I don't want to work for you anymore. I've been low down on the totem pole ever since I started, all the promises you made have never seen the light of day." He stood. "Good luck, but I'll be off now."

He walked out of the pub. Marcus staring after him with his mouth wide open. It seemed the bloke was having trouble comprehending the fact that his former employee actually had a mind of his own and had taken control of the steering wheel. Of course, it helped that he had the promise of much better wages from George and

Greg, but the man would be an asset once he'd been trained up.

Marcus turned back to his pint and managed two mouthfuls, then a server came and placed his food down. George decided to let him eat before they carted him off for questioning. He wasn't even going to bother taking him to the cottage. What had to be said could be done down an alley, as could a beating.

George sipped his Coke, and Greg played a mundane game on his phone. They hadn't let Kenny and Liz know they were in the building, these particular disguises giving them the air of people who needed a bath and their clothes could do with a damn good wash. Kenny had served them, treating them the same as any of the better-dressed customers, even going so far as to chat to them about the weather. George had known they'd picked the right couple to run the pub, but that little undercover conversation had further proved it to him, as did the fact he got a text message.

KENNY: JUST NOTICED THAT MARCUS BLOKE IS BACK IN HERE.

GG: CHEERS.

As though he'd whipped himself up into a frenzied anger, Marcus abruptly abandoned his food halfway through and stood, storming out of the pub on a mission. George and Greg rose and followed, Kenny finally twigging who they were and giving them a wink and a wave. They didn't rush, as a couple of their men were outside, one in a car and one in a Transit. By the time George had stepped onto the pavement, Marcus was nowhere in sight and the Transit was driving off. Their man in the car followed it. George and Greg leaped in their taxi and took off in pursuit, George catching sight of the vehicles a few metres ahead around the corner. George accessed an app and checked Marcus' location from where the Transit man would have put a device under his wheel arch while he'd been in the pub.

Greg flashed the headlights to tell their man in the car to turn off and finish for the day, then he put his foot down to catch up with the Transit. George leaned to the left to peer around the van. Marcus' car was still in front, although he wasn't heading in the direction of his house but the lock-up. Greg flashed the headlights again, and the Transit took the next turning, leaving the taxi to glide up behind Marcus' vehicle.

The bloke looked in his rearview mirror several times—maybe he was being paranoid about the van following and now wondered whether the taxi had taken its place. When it was clear from the app that Marcus was definitely going to the lock-up, Greg took a right and followed the road round. There was still the brother to talk to in order to see if he had knowledge the lock-up was being used for stolen goods, but then again, a phone call in his boss' ear would get an investigation going. Losing his job would be punishment enough.

Greg parked in the next street along, more of a track bordered by trees. "Can you get hold of Bennett or John and find out if there are any cameras in this lane?"

George did that, the response coming quickly. "Not here, but there are in the next street and around the lock-up. John's going to turn them off."

"Come on." Greg got out of the taxi.

George went after him up the lane and then did a quick dart left down an alley. They came out behind the lock-up perimeter fence, and as Greg seemed to know where he was going, George let him lead without asking any questions. They emerged at the edge of the customer car park.

Marcus's car pulled up, and he popped his motor between a Kia and an Escort, getting out and taking a couple of steps towards the reception building.

"Oi," Greg whispered loudly. "Can you help me?"

Marcus stopped and stared over. "Go to reception, someone will help you there."

"I can't walk that far." Greg staggered backwards and deliberately fell onto his arse, well away from the reach of any camera lens. "Oh Jesus Christ, my chest hurts…"

Marcus couldn't be too bad a person because he rushed forward and crouched, gripping the top of one of Greg's arms to help him stand. George took his opportunity and created a double fist, bringing it down on the back of Marcus' head. The man's grunt of surprise pierced the darkness, and he landed over Greg, then scrambled to get up. George gripped the back of Marcus' coat, lifted him enough to stuff a rag from his pocket in his mouth, then hauled him to his feet and dragged him back down the alley towards the taxi. He bundled him in the back and got in there with him, sitting on the puny bastard to keep him still. Greg got in the driver's seat and drove away.

"You know you said to Moody you thought the meeting in the pub was a trap?" George asked.

A groan came from beneath him.

George smiled. "You were right."

* * * *

Mad had come out to play, much to George's surprise and delight, but it meant they now had the problem of a dead body to deal with. Mad had gone a bit too far, and the result was likely lots of broken bones beneath the bruised skin.

"Fucking hell," Greg said. "I told you to stop, but you wouldn't listen."

"You know what I get like when Mad comes for a visit."

"It's been a while since I've had to step in and pull you off of someone, so I'll take the blame because I should have been more vigilant. I should never have believed Mad had learned how to control himself—or *you'd* learned how to control him."

George ignored that. "So what we going to do with this numpty, then?" He gestured to a very dead Marcus on the ground behind a deserted building.

"It'll have to be the cottage, but we've got limited space under there, as you well know. With the warehouse now out of action…" Greg paused. "Hang on a minute. Have you switched on your personal phone lately?"

"Not that I recall."

"So no missed calls or messages from the Old Bill about the fact that our warehouse has burned down to the ground and Colin hasn't said a fucking word. What's that all about?"

"The phone thing is easy. We don't have contracts, and the police don't know what our numbers are. We haven't been home much so they've probably been to our house to tell us the news, found we were out, and fucked off again. As for Colin not telling us, he works on the murder squad, not arson, so why *would* he know?"

"Fair enough, I just thought it was a bit strange, that's all. Not one person mentioned the warehouse going up in flames when we were at the fayre earlier. You'd think shit like that would spread."

"Maybe they thought that's why we were at the fayre, on the lookout for who torched it. I expect when we do eventually speak to the police, they'll suspect us of doing a fraudulent insurance claim and want to know where we were, all that bollocks, but with all the cameras being offline, there's no proof we were in the vicinity at all. Anyway, we'll deal with that when we have to."

"But don't you think the police will think it's a bit weird that we haven't heard about the fire yet or enquired with the authorities about it, considering we're supposed to be using it as a business property."

"They've more than likely discovered there was nothing of significance inside apart from burnt tools, but yeah, we should really nip by there, see it's burnt down, and then pop into the local nick to ask why we weren't told about it. Fuck's sake, that's all we need on top of this. So back to this twat. What are we doing?"

"Sod the cottage. We'll stick him in his car and leave him there, then get John to switch the cameras back on half an hour after we've left.

Marcus is a thief, and if the police ask questions about his beating, people will grass him up for it now there'll be no repercussions because he's dead."

"It could be put down to the church theft, though. Residents know we bought those televisions."

Greg let out a long sigh. "Why does everything have to be so fucking difficult? Help me carry him back to the taxi."

They bundled him in the boot and drove off, George annoyed that blood would be in the vehicle, so they'd have to get their cleaning crew to valet it, not to mention they still hadn't come up with a solid plan.

"What are we doing?" he asked. "I sense you've changed your mind about his car."

"We're going to have to nip home first so I can get the van and follow you to the cottage. We'll drop him off and dump him under the steel room, then leave the taxi somewhere the crew can get it cleaned up. We'll go home in the van, get showered, burn our clothes, and collect the taxi later."

George nodded, and Greg drove on.

Chapter Twenty-Eight

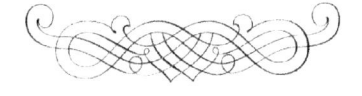

Miss Marchant had quite the posh little house. How she afforded it, Ruffian didn't know, but she'd done well for herself. He prowled around the ground floor, his torch beam on low, snooping in cupboards and drawers. Everywhere smelled of lemon polish, reminding him of Mum when she'd been round with her yellow dusting cloth. An unexpected stab of tears pricked the backs of his eyes, and he blinked them away, reminding himself he had no time for sentimentality, the same as when he'd taken the wooden chair out of the warehouse. He'd burned it before coming here and still had the smell of smoke in his nostrils. Maybe Miss Marchant would smell it soon, too; the scent had also stuck to his clothes.

He shouldn't really leave Greg outside in the van for too long, despite this being a four-house cul-de-sac. Everyone had seemed to be in bed when they'd arrived, all the homes in darkness.

"Fucking hot in here," he muttered.

Miss Marchant clearly left the heating on overnight so could afford the cost, unlike many of the residents on the Cardigan Estate. His face sweated beneath the wool of the balaclava, as did his palms under the gloves, but they were a necessary evil. He couldn't leave fingerprints nor let her see his face.

He climbed the stairs and paused at the top, pointing his torch beam towards the floor and moving it along so he could count how many doors were on the landing. Five, so three bedrooms, a bathroom, and an airing cupboard.

All of them were closed, so he'd have to open each one to check where the gossiping bitch was. He found her in the third one along and crept into her room, standing on her side of the bed, bending low so that when she woke, his face was right above hers. He gripped a gun in his right hand, propped the torch on her nightstand, then held his other hand up, ready to slap it across her mouth—she was probably going to scream when she saw him.

"Wakey, wakey," he said in a Scottish accent.

Her eyes flicked open quickly and widened at the sight of him. Her lips parted, and he lowered his leather-gloved palm and pressed down on her mouth. Before she had the chance to struggle, he pushed the business end of the gun to her temple.

"I hear you've been gossiping about that wee lad who got killed," he murmured. "I also hear that George said 'You'll keep'. Do you want to know how I know that? Because I was at the fayre. I was listening. I was watching. I killed Jason, and I could kill you in the same way, except I want to give you a chance to behave yourself first."

She whimpered and made an attempt at a nod, but his hand clamped over her mouth held her head against the pillow.

"Are you trying to tell me you're going to be a good girl now?"

"Hmm, hmm."

"I'll take that as a yes then." He put the gun in the holster beneath his jacket and got on top of her, holding her arms down with his knees, keeping his palm across her lower face and placing his other around her throat. He didn't put too much pressure on her Adam's apple, instead creating the bruises he needed by digging in his thumb and fingertips.

Her eyes filled with tears, but he had no sympathy for her, just like she'd had no sympathy for Jason and Kathleen Ludlow. This fucking chatty cow had thought nothing of discussing that lad's death with anyone who'd listen. Maybe this little episode would teach her to keep her opinions to herself in future. Maybe it would knock that chip off her shoulder George so despised.

He took his hand from her neck to pull a cable tie out of his pocket. He punched her in the face three times to subdue her—all right, and to break her beaky nose—and while she was in shock and whimpering, he took his hand away from her mouth in order to cable tie her wrists together. He got off her and stood by the bed, flinging her over onto her front, pressing her face into her pillow—she wasn't to know this was only a threat to suffocate her. He pushed harder to make her think she was going to die, at the same time reaching across to open the top drawer of her bedside cabinet. Inside were neatly rolled knickers, so he took two pairs out, squeezed them together, then wrenched her head up by the hair and stuffed them in her mouth.

He flipped her over onto her back, collected his torch and shone it right in her eyes. "Remember me the next time you fancy starring in your own show. Remember that I might hear about it and come back for you, like I came back for Jason because he saw me taking those televisions. Now you lie there and think about what you've done while I go downstairs."

He popped the torch away and took another cable tie out and slid the pointed end through the loop of the one around her wrist. He secured it to the strut of her iron headboard, then exited the room. Downstairs in the living room, he peered out of the window at the side of the curtain to check the quiet street. All clear, he left the house and got in the van.

"What took you so long?" Greg grumbled and drove away.

"I was having a wee nose around."

"Oh great. And meanwhile, I was out here and could have got seen."

"Even if you did, you're in disguise and the van's got a fake number plate, so shut your mouth. Come on, it's time to go home. I fancy getting a kebab delivered."

"You do realise you actually spoke this whole conversation in a Scottish accent, don't you?"

George blinked. "Och aye the noo."

Greg tutted. "Dickhead."

Chapter Twenty-Nine

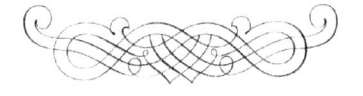

Betty stood in a nondescript hotel room opposite her son who was more of a stranger now. She *felt* the chasm between them, how it stretched so wide and seemed impossible to reach across. Maybe one day it wouldn't be there anymore, when he came out on the other side of his addiction, but with the guilt he would experience if he went back to being the old Ezra, she imagined he might well not want to ever face her again, because facing her meant facing shame and his sins.

She liked to think her expression showed him she'd forgive him anything, but unfortunately, he'd hurt her too much and too often for her to be one of those mothers who loved her child without any caveats. They were there whether she liked it or not. She'd chosen herself over him lately, unwilling to let him treat her like shit, and she'd come to see that it wasn't a bad thing that she take care of her own mental health rather than pandering to her son's every greedy, grasping whim. Although that was the drugs talking, she was sure of it, but still, he'd made a conscious decision to call her names, to use her, to abuse her, so no, she didn't love him unconditionally.

He seemed nervous, as though he didn't know what to say or that he worried the wrong thing would come out of his mouth. George and Greg had explained to her where he was going and that he'd be attending university up north as well as working and living there for a man they knew called Jimmy. She dreaded to think who that was and didn't ask. Surely, a life away from London was better than the life Ezra had lived while here. Providing he could stay off the drugs, he may well make something of himself yet.

It didn't matter to her whether he had a big career with a fancy car and he swanned around in suits that cost more than a week's wages. What mattered was that he was happy, healthy, and their relationship could be healed at least so they were civil to each other. Mind you, she had to give herself a pat on the back because for ninety-five percent of the time she'd been polite to him despite how he'd treated her. She'd been the bigger person, the adult, and he the child, much as he wouldn't see it that way yet. He had a lot of growing to do before he understood his actions had been immature. Still, she wouldn't rub it in his face. Maybe never would. It was time to let him go and then she could get on with her life without him.

"I didn't mean half the shit I said," he blurted.

She smiled. "Only half?"

"I mean most of the shit. All of it."

"You must have meant it to have said it at the time, but we'll say that was heroin's voice, not yours, shall we?"

He nodded. "I don't know why it all went so wrong. When I turned into such a little cunt. It wasn't me, was it? Before I met that lot, I'd never have spoken to you like that."

She didn't say that before he'd taken the drugs he wouldn't have done it either, but it was there in the air between them just the same, lingering. "The important thing is that you want to fix yourself now, before it's too late. Those televisions and poor Jason being killed, that was all Kash. If it wasn't for him, you wouldn't have gone with him to the church that night, Jason wouldn't have seen you, and Kash wouldn't have ended up killing him."

Ezra had confided in her via text that he had witnessed Kash stabbing Jason. She'd promised to keep it a secret, or at least pretend she hadn't known about it if Ezra finally confessed to the twins. It was going to be a difficult task. She felt Kash needed to be punished.

"They'll deal with him," she said. "They'll work out who it was eventually, they always do."

"It's a good job I owned up to a few things then. They'd have only caught me otherwise, and there's no way they'd be sending me up north and finding me a job and whatever."

He didn't have to say that it was because she knew them that they'd gone lenient and above and beyond for her son. Those unspoken words lingered, too, joining the million others neither of them were ready to say just yet. But Betty wanted to say them, she wanted to blurt all of them out so he went away knowing she'd never stopped loving him, she'd just stopped liking him for a little while. But even then, saying the latter would put a dampener on things, a negative spin, and now they were at least in the same room and weren't at loggerheads, she preferred to keep things cordial. She had Lainey to talk to about her gripes, and once Ezra had been taken away in one of the twins' cars for the north, she'd go home and cry her heart out with her next-door neighbour over a Chinese and a bottle of wine.

"Do you ever wonder what I'd have been like if I hadn't met Kash and everybody?"

She was going to have to lie. "No."

He smiled but quickly erased it, worry seeping into his expression. "What if I can't get clean? What if the methadone and all that stuff doesn't work?"

She had the urge to touch him, to squeeze his arm, but he was too far away and she didn't want to invade his space. "It's one step at a time. Don't worry about things that haven't happened yet."

A tap at the door had her tensing because it was time for goodbye. Just because it was a good thing, what was happening, it didn't mean it wasn't going to hurt. Yes, he'd left home already, but that had been under a dark cloud. This time it was under a white one, the sunshine obscured until he dealt with everything he needed to, but then there'd be blue skies again.

"I love you," she said and turned away from him to go towards the door so she didn't have to see him rolling his eyes or his lips not moving where he didn't say it back. As long as he knew how she felt, she could walk out of here with no regrets. She gripped the handle and twisted it.

"I love you, too, and I *am* sorry, you know."

"I know. Text me or ring me anytime."

Again she didn't turn. She didn't want to see his face, nor did she want him to see hers. She was on the verge of ugly crying. She opened the door and stepped into the hallway, blinking the tears away and lifting a hand of acknowledgment to George and Greg. Then she stumbled down the carpeted corridor and around the corner to the lift. She prodded the button and counted down the floors. The lift arrived, and she got on, and, enclosed in the metal box, she burst into tears, relieved that at last this was all over. Even if it was only all over *for now*, the situation had better prospects than what had been on offer a couple of days ago.

Her hidden emotions emerged, surging through her, a great wave she couldn't control. She let out a few ragged sobs, then got a hold of herself and tucked her feelings away, having to rebury them once again so she could present as a normal, functioning human being. Ezra would be okay. This Jimmy would look after him. He'd do well and he'd stay clean forever, maybe meet a girl and have a family.

These hopes were all too big at the moment, like she'd said to him, one step at a time, but she secretly thought that you never knew where life could take you until you dared to imagine, so call her a woman with her head in the clouds, but she was going to dream.

Chapter Thirty

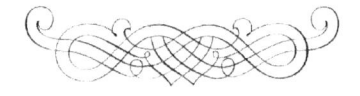

Kash hadn't been out of the hospital for long. His mum and dad had bought tickets to a party in the King's Arms before he'd been hurt, and they'd still gone out for it even though Mum had said she'd stay behind and keep him company. To be honest, she'd spent a lot of time in the hospital with him after his knee operations, and at this point she was getting right on his tits. He loved her but didn't need her in his face, and Dad was just as bad, fretting and worrying every time Kash needed to go to the toilet. He'd got the hang of using both crutches and swinging himself along to the little loo. They'd made a bedroom for him in the dining room, which meant they'd cancelled the visitors coming for Christmas as there wouldn't be enough room for everyone to sit and eat dinner.

For once he actually felt bad for disrupting things, *and* for the fact they'd used their savings to pay off the rent he'd owed right up until the end of the two months' notice he'd given. Dad had gone in with his mate and emptied the place, and Mum had used her Vax to clean all the carpets. Now there was just the wait to see whether Kash would get the bond returned.

It was Christmas Eve, and there was a load of the usual shite on normal telly, so he switched over to watch a new series on Netflix. Had he still lived with the lads, they'd probably be getting stoned and high and watching it together tonight. Rory and Ollie must have blocked his phone number because when he sent them messages earlier they didn't go through, and as for Ezra, he didn't respond either.

It was weird because it was Rory who'd got the lot of them into drugs, yet it seemed Kash was the one getting the cold shoulder for it. He'd been a good kid once, until he'd met up with them, just like Ezra had been. Kash had wanted to warn Ezra to stay away from them, to not get involved, saying his life would never be the same, but he'd shrugged and told himself the kid could make his own decisions.

Everything had gone so wrong. At least while he'd been in hospital he'd got some help for his addiction. For some reason, he'd always been able to give or take heroin. It was the coke he struggled to go without, not to mention the marijuana. Those days spent on that ward where nothing was available had given him the perfect opportunity to quit. He'd gone cold turkey, and his head was a lot clearer and he could finally see a way out of the fog.

There were times in the middle of the night when he woke up screaming, except the screams were silent in the house but loud inside his head. He was in the woods with a knife, and he'd gone there with the intent to kill Jason, to eliminate him from being a witness to the robbery. It turned out he needn't have bothered, but at the time he'd panicked. If he could turn the clock back on that one, he would. Dad had mentioned the twins had been round when Kash was still in hospital. They'd asked when he'd be out so they could come and see him and wish him well. Kash knew that wasn't what they'd really be doing, they'd visit him to make sure he kept his mouth shut about the kneecapping, but he wasn't about to tell his old man that, nor his mother.

The front doorbell rang. It would have to go ignored because by the time he got up and to the hallway, whoever it was would have fucked off. Besides, he was sick to death of carol singers, usually teenagers after money so they could go and buy themselves one of those throwaway vapes. He turned the telly up and hoped they got the message to fuck off.

The bell didn't ring again, so he snuggled down in his single bed, his eyes drooping as he tried to focus on the television. Something tapped to his right, possibly that stupid fir tree in the garden, its branches whacking and scraping on the glass of the back door. He didn't bother to pull the curtain across to check, just closed his eyes and hoped for oblivion.

When he woke, the television was off, the room in complete darkness. The thud of his heartbeat was so loud in his ears, overlaid with the harshness of his breathing. He panted, panic tightening his chest, then he remembered where he was, his childhood home, and that Mum had probably come in after the party and switched his telly off. But it felt like someone was there with him. They could be far away or they could be close, he couldn't tell because it was so pitch-black, but he swore the air buzzed with their presence.

"Some people, no matter what promises they make, have an attack of conscience and end up coming to us to sort it out."

The sound of the whispered voice, the recognisable tone, had Kash holding his breath and his bladder threatening to empty. He should have known this day would come, that they wouldn't knock on the front door like normal people. He glanced towards the end of his bed to check the time, but the glowing numbers of his digital clock were missing. Had they turned it off before he woke?

"Ezra's mum told him she'd keep a secret, but she couldn't do it, not when Jason's killer is still out there and his poor gran just wants his murderer caught. We should have twigged it was you anyway when our surveillance bloke saw you turn up in your street to talk to the man with the flatbed lorry. I mean, what would you have been doing out at that time of night?"

Kash wasn't sure whether he was supposed to answer that so remained silent.

"Ezra's never going to know his mum gave up his secret. That kid's got enough on his plate to deal with. What he *is* going to find out, though, is that you're dead and we worked it out that you killed Jason. Anyway, in half an hour it's going to click over to midnight and it'll be Christmas Day. When your parents come back, they're going to find an almighty present in this bed, one they'll never forget. I'm going to kill you the same way you killed Jason, and I'm going to leave you the way you left Jason. You'll bleed out all on your own, but at least you'll be warm and have a comfy mattress to die on. He was cold and bled out on the ground, you absolute despicable piece of scum. When news spreads that you've been murdered, our copper will make sure the killer's never found, and then me and my brother will come here and offer your parents some money for a funeral, acting like we give a shit, when all along, I'm the one who killed you."

The bite of the blade going into the side of his neck stole Kash's breath. He'd heard you didn't feel a knife going in until a few seconds later, but that was a lie, he felt the whole slide. Blood welled in his throat, and he coughed and spluttered. He had the vague notion that if the blade stayed where it was he might very well survive, but then movement at his neck and agonising pain told him the steel was being removed. The hot, wet heat of blood going down his throat and onto his shoulders, the smell of it…he wanted to be sick. He coughed again, the pain unbearable, then came the cool waft of a winter night's draught as George left the dining room via the back door, the muted clunk when he locked it.

Kash closed his eyes and willed himself to die quickly, his body convulsing, memories from his life flashing, his final thought that of his poor mother finding his body and how, once again, he'd caused her immeasurable agony.

Chapter Thirty-One

The red scarf draped around her neck caught his attention immediately. He stared at it, then the woman, to see if she was one of those with enough money to be able to afford something from Fusion Fashions. The boutique had been high-end and not exactly for those living on a tight budget. Having said that, it didn't mean the women themselves were high-end. Jodie Swain had been a prostitute, one of the others a cashier, the third an administrative assistant, and the latest one, Libby, he never was sure what she did, if anything. Before he'd been sent away, he hadn't really had a chance to properly stalk her.

He followed the flash of scarlet through the crowd, weaving between people who'd come out for the New Year sales, those greedy for a bargain. He drew closer to his target, and with a startling dose of clarity, he realised the scarf wasn't the same. It had a hand-knitted look to it but wasn't the one from Fusion Fashions. And the colour was slightly wrong, not quite the same shade.

Still, it had stirred his blood, giving him a taste for another rape and kill, but he'd promised himself Libby was the final one, she always had been. After all, he'd only ever had those four women in mind, there had never been plans for number five. While he'd been away, he'd thought about what he'd done—how could he not?—and wished he'd completed the foursome in time. Had Libby not been unfinished business, he'd never have killed her when he'd come back.

Four was the limit for the Red Scarf Mission, but it didn't mean he couldn't choose another item to focus on. He glanced around the crowd in the busy high street and noted a specific shade of green seemed to be a popular colour. Bright. Striking. Shamrock #03AC13 if he was any judge, or maybe Parakeet #03C04A. He'd check his colour palette later.

Did he have the time and energy for another mission? And as there were so many different colours of green in this crowd, could he afford to be so picky like he had with the red (Candy #D21404)? Did everyone have to have exactly the same coat or hat or handbag from the same shop? Not really. The Red Scarf Mission had been easy because there was only one Fusion Fashions, but times had changed with so many shops around now, so much to choose from, and the explosion that was online shopping.

He lost sight of the red scarf, and lost interest in the woman who wore it, his gaze now drawn to a lady in a fitted Shamrock coat—yes, definitely Shamrock now he'd had a closer look. Belted at the waist, it appeared to be made from a wool blend, the collar wide, the buttons black to match her long hair. Had she had a nice

Christmas? Did she have a family who waited for her at home? That would be awkward. He'd prefer it if she lived alone. She broke from the crowd, striding off in her knee-high black boots, her black leather handbag swinging beside her. She looked expensive, as if her whole outfit had cost a month's wages. Maybe they'd been Christmas presents. Or maybe she had a good job and could afford them herself.

All things he could find out if he was prepared to go on another mission.

Was he?

As the first few plops of rain descended, she darted into a coffee shop. That wasn't a bad idea, actually, he could do with a latte. He drew his hood over his head and dashed across the street, dipping inside the café, too. That was the thing with colours, they drew the eye, got you noticed, and there she was, in all her Shamrock glory, highly noticeable, easily picked out from the masses. He, on the other hand, opted for the darker shade of things.

Was that green coat going to be her downfall?

He wasn't sure yet.

He sat at the table next to hers and waited for someone to come and take his order. She smelled nice; he was almost certain it was Lady Million, a distinctive scent that stood out whenever he sniffed the testers in the chemist. She placed her bag on the table and took her phone out, then glanced up and smiled at the waitress. He imagined doing what he shouldn't by ignoring her right to say no. He imagined using the coat belt around her neck as she lay on the grass, struggling to breathe.

His one regret had been dealing with Libby in her house. It was the only time he'd acted on his urges when he shouldn't. He'd crept around the side of her house and seen her in the garden, where there was plenty of grass he could have taken her on, but it had been summer and light out, and someone would have seen him from the windows of the neighbouring houses. And besides, she'd run indoors at the sight of him, probably in search of her phone.

He dragged himself out of his head and into the present. The woman ordered a coffee, a cheese sandwich, and a piece of chocolate cake. He'd do the same, eating and drinking in sync with her—she'd lift her cup, so would he; she'd bite into her sandwich crust, so would he. Then he'd follow her out of here and begin the process—if, of course, he decided to go ahead with it. He told himself he still wasn't sure, but deep down, he knew he'd already made the decision.

She didn't have much longer to live.

The be continued in *Repudiate*,
The Cardigan Estate 36

Printed in Great Britain
by Amazon